W9-DCH-940

"You were married?" he asked in surprise

"Briefly." Vanessa looked away from the curiosity lighting his eyes.

"You must have been young."

"Nineteen—a very young nineteen."

Shane studied the curve of her averted face. "If you want to tell me it's none of my business, feel free. But—what happened?"

"Our views on fidelity clashed badly. He told me he was going to a party one night. He neglected to tell me it was a private party for two."

"It must have been rough." His hand touched her arm gently.

"It was awful. But it was my mistake to ever marry a man like that in the first place."

"Marriage is a mistake a lot of people make," he added with certainty.

"Do you speak from experience?"

"No," he said curtly. "And I never plan to."

Samantha Day, a Canadian author, used to work in a school library but now makes romance writing her full-time occupation. Having perfected the art of daydreaming, she says she learned how to transcribe what she saw in her mind onto sheets of blank paper. Her husband and daughter are wonderfully supportive and encouraging of her romance writing.

Books by Samantha Day

HARLEQUIN ROMANCE
2672—THE TURN OF THE TIDE
2840—FOR KARIN'S SAKE

Don't miss any of our special offers. Write to us at the following address for information on our newest releases.

Harlequin Reader Service
901 Fuhrmann Blvd., P.O. Box 1397, Buffalo, NY 14240
Canadian address: P.O. Box 603,
Fort Erie, Ont. L2A 5X3

There Must Be Love

Samantha Day

Harlequin Books

TORONTO • NEW YORK • LONDON
AMSTERDAM • PARIS • SYDNEY • HAMBURG
STOCKHOLM • ATHENS • TOKYO • MILAN

ISBN 0-373-02923-3

Harlequin Romance first edition August 1988

With thanks to Chantal
for Bertie Butterbug

Copyright © 1988 by Sandra Courcelles.
Cover illustration copyright © 1988 by Will Davies.
All rights reserved. Except for use in any review, the reproduction or utilization
of this work in whole or in part in any form by any electronic, mechanical or
other means, now known or hereafter invented, including xerography,
photocopying and recording, or in any information storage or retrieval system,
is forbidden without the permission of the publisher, Harlequin Enterprises
Limited, 225 Duncan Mill Road, Don Mills, Ontario, Canada M3B 3K9.

All the characters in this book have no existence outside the imagination of
the author and have no relation whatsoever to anyone bearing the same name
or names. They are not even distantly inspired by any individual known or
unknown to the author, and all incidents are pure invention.

® are Trademarks registered in the United States Patent and Trademark Office
and in other countries.

Printed in U.S.A.

CHAPTER ONE

VANESSA BRIEFLY LOOKED UP from the page as she caught a glimpse of a tall male figure standing by the library door, then continued reading.

"'And to thank you, Bertie Butterbug,' Mother Nature said. 'You and all the other Butterbugs shall have wings as varied and as colorful as the flowers. You will no longer be Butterbugs but Butterflies!'"

She closed the book and smiled at the children sitting cross-legged on the floor in front of her. "That's it, kids. Did you like the story?"

"Yes!" The young voices chorused enthusiastically.

"Good. You can go and choose your books now. Remember," she called as the children began to scramble toward the wooden shelves lined with picture books. "Print your names on the card in the back of the book and today's date, which is?"

"October twenty-second!" A few children still paying attention responded.

"That's right. Then return the card to me. If you need any help, just ask me." She watched them for a moment, smiling at their eagerness, and then turned her attention to the doorway. The intruder was leaning against the wall just inside the entry, arms crossed over his chest as he watched the roomful of buzzing children.

"Can I help you?" Vanessa asked, walking toward him. She wondered if he might be a substitute sent to cover for one of the full-time teachers.

"I hope so." He grinned as he straightened, his thickly lashed light gray eyes friendly. "Tell me—how did Bertie Butterbug earn his wings?"

Vanessa returned his smile easily. "He and all the other Butterbugs planted flower seeds for Mother Nature to brighten up a drab world. She gave them wings to thank them." She smiled again. "Is that all, or can I help you with something else?"

"Actually," he said, his deep voice a lazy drawl, "I'm here to help you."

Vanessa's eyebrows rose slightly. "Colliers, World Book or Britannica?"

He smiled lazily. "I'm not selling. I'm volunteering."

"For what?"

"Whatever you want me for." The way he smiled as he studied her face made Vanessa feel slightly uncomfortable.

"You are Ms Evans, aren't you?"

"I am," she said with a slight frown. "And you are?"

"Wilder," he answered briefly.

"Than what?" She was unable to resist the the response.

His eyes flashed and his smile widened. "Shane Wilder—actually quite tame and usually harmless. I read about the lack of volunteers in the schools in this area, and I have some free time on my hands each day, so—" He shrugged. "Here I am."

Vanessa glanced over his lithe, lean frame, the wide expanse of shoulders and his self-assured stance, skeptically. Her doubts showed plainly.

"Is there a problem?" he asked.

"It's just—" Vanessa hesitated and then lifted her shoulders and spoke honestly. "You don't look like the usual volunteer."

"And you don't look like the usual librarian," he returned, an appreciative gleam in his eyes as they swept lazily over her delicate frame. "Not from what I remember, anyway. Are you—"

"Teacher!" A plaintive voice interrupted him. "I wanted that book but Tanya got it and she won't give it to me!"

Brown eyes gazed up at Vanessa, who turned her attention instantly to the child. "Well, Binh, let's go see if there's another copy of that story. If not, I'm sure we can find one you'll like just as much." She took the small hand in hers, then turned toward the man briefly. "Feel free to look around, Mr. Wilder. I'll be able to talk to you after this class, in about ten minutes or so."

As Vanessa helped the children find books and sign them out, she caught glimpses of Shane Wilder out of the corner of her eye. After he'd had a quick look around the large, bright room with its shelves of books and display tables, he started talking easily to some of the children. She saw him hunkering down beside a child-size worktable, asking questions of a boy eagerly leafing through a book on dinosaurs. When a young girl asked the man how to sign out her book, he guided her through the steps instead of doing it for her. Before long he was surrounded by several children, all vying for his attention, quick to sense his interest.

Vanessa turned away with a little grimace of dismay. For some reason she had hoped that the noise and confusion of sign-out time would make him think twice about volunteering but, if anything, it looked as if his short time with the children would encourage him to help out. Certainly he seemed to be enjoying himself.

When the classroom teacher returned to the library, the children, clutching their books, lined up dutifully. "Thank you, Ms Evans," they chorused on cue from their teacher and filed out of the room.

Vanessa walked toward the man examining one of the displays, a colorful collection of stories and pictures done by a grade-three class based on the fairy tales she had been reading to them during library period.

"So, Mr. Wilder," she said, "are you still interested in volunteering?"

"Very much so," he answered, turning to her. "What would I be doing?"

"First, I need some information from you. Just the basic stuff," she said, trying to sound casual while being cautious.

"I've already talked to the principal," Shane said. "She seemed satisfied. She was going to come down and introduce me, but was held up by a phone call."

Vanessa nodded. Bettina Blakely was a quick and shrewd judge of character. If she had any doubts at all about this man, he wouldn't have got this far. "All right," she said. "But tell me, Mr. Wilder—what are your reasons for wanting to do volunteer work in an elementary school? Do you have children here?"

He shook his head. "No, no children. I'm not married. I work at home," he continued. "It's quiet and peaceful and inclined to be—well, stifling after a while." He shrugged. "I need more contact with the real world. And after reading that article about the lack of volunteers in inner-city schools, I decided to make myself available. And this school's convenient for me. So here I am." He looked around the room. "A library isn't quite what I had in mind, but," he added, his eyes widening as they met hers, "I don't think I'm going to mind."

Vanessa heard a flirtatious note in his voice and looked again at the clear, smiling eyes, his strong, handsome face. He didn't look the type of man who'd want to commit himself to anything for long. Perhaps if she had him doing something clerical rather than working directly with a child he'd become restless sooner and stop coming? Why didn't she want this man in her library? Just because he happened to be attractive didn't mean he couldn't be a good volunteer.

"There are several things you could do," she began slowly. "There is a rather large stack of books that need to be repaired, or—"

"I hope the 'or' is something to do with kids," he interrupted. "I spend a lot of time sitting quietly—I need something more stimulating than taping torn pages." His eyes narrowed slightly as if he sensed some of her hesitation. "I'm not here on a whim, Ms Evans," he said assuredly. "I'm serious about this."

"Good," she said, putting aside some of her doubts. "The school would love to have someone with the time to come in and work with a few of the problem children, but we need a promise of commitment." She looked at him resolvedly. "A lot of these kids come from rather—well, chaotic backgrounds. They need the school to be a stable, dependable environment. If we put you to work with one of them, we'd expect you to come regularly, preferably until the end of the year."

"That's no problem," he said easily. "I can give a couple of hours, say, two afternoons a week?" He looked at her, his eyes suddenly intense. "I can understand the need for continuity in a kid's life, Ms Evans. And, like I said, I'm serious about this."

Vanessa looked at him closely for a moment and then nodded. Whatever his reasons for doing this, he did seem sincere and while personally she might have her doubts, professionally she knew she had to accept whatever time and skill he had to offer. "What I'd like to do, Mr. Wilder, is—"

"Shane," he interrupted.

She blinked. "What?"

He grinned at her. "Call me Shane."

"All right—Shane," she agreed a little reluctantly. "Now—"

"What shall I call you?" he interrupted again.

Vanessa gave a half smile. "Ms Evans."

"Come on," he coaxed, his eyes gleaming with laughter. "What's your first name?"

"Sometimes after a day with the kids, I start thinking it's Teacher. But it's Vanessa."

"Vanessa," he repeated, reaching out for a handshake. "It's a beautiful name. It suits you."

"Thank you," Vanessa replied, extending her hand cautiously. His hand was warm and firm, the palm just slightly rough. His fingers tightened around hers briefly and then released immediately. It was a courteous handshake, the kind she'd share with anyone, but somehow he had managed to make it feel flirtatious. It's his eyes, she thought stealing another quick glance at him. They were such knowing eyes, brimming with lazy amusement. "Now, Mr.—Shane—are you sure you want to sacrifice that much of your time?"

"I'm sure," he said firmly. "I work for a few hours every morning and my afternoons are usually free. I want to spend them doing something worthwhile."

"What do you do?" she asked curiously.

"I'm a writer," he said.

The book lover in Vanessa responded instantly. "What do you write?" she asked, unable to hide her enthusiasm.

"Detective novels," he responded nonchalantly.

"Oh." There was a note of disappointment in her voice as she saw a flash of a garish book cover complete with buxom blonde and blood-dripping knife at her neck. "Have you been published?" she asked.

"Many times," he drawled, amused by the look of surprise on her face. "You mean you haven't read about the continuing exploits of Matt Savage, Private Eye?"

Vanessa shook her head and smiled apologetically. "No. Sorry."

He waved a hand dismissingly. "Well—they aren't for everyone. Besides, most of my fans are men, anyway. Now, what can I do to help out here?—along with repairing books, of course." He smiled.

She ignored the playful gibe and continued. "We want to start a special reading program," Vanessa explained. "A one-on-one thing, to turn certain kids on to reading."

Shane chuckled suddenly. "I like it—training future fans. Do you have a particular child in mind?"

Vanessa mentally reviewed the list of children the staff had considered for the program. "Tommy Hawkes, I think," she said finally. Tommy lived alone with his mother and would benefit from the masculine attention as much as anything. She looked at Shane and nodded. "Yes, definitely Tommy."

Shane's eyes narrowed with interest. "What's he like?"

"Tommy's a great kid, quiet and easygoing, and—well, not slow, but just not in any hurry. He just hasn't had much encouragement from the home front."

"What would I be doing with him?"

"In some ways it will be up to you. We want to get him reading, interested in books. Like a lot of the kids in the school, he comes from a home where books are almost nonexistent—no bedtime stories or quiet reading time. Nothing, really, to show them that reading can be fun, exciting and not just something they have to do. We want to change that."

"So when do I begin?"

"Well, we'll have to talk to his teacher first, and to Mrs. Blakely. I think I'll be able to catch them during recess." Vanessa wasn't going to commit herself further until she had talked to Bettina. As anxious as she was to get the reading program underway, she wanted to be absolutely sure Shane Wilder was the right person for the job. "I've got one more class before recess. Can you stay around for a while? You can wait in the staff room. There should be fresh coffee ready."

"Are you going to read another story?" Shane asked.

"Yes, I am. Why?"

"Can I stay and listen? I like the way you tell stories."

"Are you sure you wouldn't rather go have a cup of coffee?" Vanessa asked as a class of nine-year-olds filed in behind their teacher.

"I'm sure."

Vanessa looked at him doubtfully. "Well, okay—find a seat." She turned her attention to the students. "Good afternoon, boys and girls."

"Good afternoon, Ms Evans," they chorused raggedly.

"Go sit in the story corner." She smiled at them. "I'll be there in a minute." She saw Shane seat himself near the doorway, leaning forward on the chair, his elbows resting on his knees.

The classroom teacher, Carla Santos, stared at him with undisguised interest. "Who's the hunk?" she whispered.

"A volunteer," Vanessa answered briefly.

"He can volunteer in my room any time," Carla said. "If I wasn't dying for a cigarette, I'd go over and introduce myself. On the other hand, a couple of quick puffs should tide me over until recess. I'll be back in a couple of minutes." She left with a little wave of her fingers, smiling widely at Shane as she passed.

Shane, Vanessa noticed as she sat on a low stool in front of the expectant children, returned the smile wholeheartedly, turning to watch as Carla sauntered out the door. Turning back to find Vanessa watching him, he grinned unabashedly and leaned back in the chair, crossing his arms over his chest. Vanessa quickly directed her attention to the children, suddenly feeling a stirring of resentment at his intrusion into her library.

She sat on the low stool, slender ankles neatly crossed, holding the book at an angle so the children could see the pictures as she read. Her voice was low and melodic, her inflections sufficiently varied to keep the young listeners interested.

Vanessa knew Shane was watching her, his intent stare making her feel uncomfortable. Nervously she brushed back a strand of hair that had escaped from her soft chignon, struggling to keep her mind on the story. As she neared the end of the book, she saw Carla come back and pull up a chair next to Shane. Over the sound of her own voice, Vanessa could hear the murmur of their conversation and

Carla's sudden muffled laughter. She turned slightly and could see Shane leaning toward Carla, listening attentively to what she was saying.

Vanessa hoped her displeasure didn't show. He was taking as much interest in Carla as he had taken in her. The man's a flirt, she decided. Finishing the story, she dismissed the children to choose their books.

Carla continued talking to Shane despite the continual interruptions of her students. She couldn't really blame Carla. Shane Wilder was a very attractive man. Dark curls tumbled around his head in attractive disorder, framing his strong-boned face. High cheekbones narrowed to a jutting jaw with a chin cut by a hint of a cleft. Dimples quivered in the corners of his well-shaped mouth. His heavy-lidded and thickly lashed gray eyes gleamed constantly with a natural lazy amusement.

Vanessa might have found him attractive but for that come-hither look in his eyes. He had the look of a philanderer, she noted cynically, and she'd had enough of that kind of man with Todd. Good looks in a man accounted for very little, she had decided long ago. She wanted dependability, someone who could be counted on, someone who would stay faithful and loving.

"Is it always busy like this?" Shane asked as Carla led the the noisy class out of the room. "I thought libraries were quiet places."

Vanessa smiled. "Not this one. Most days it's like a zoo in here. Are you still sure you'll be able to stand it?"

He nodded decisively. "Yeah—this could be just the thing for me. When do I meet Tommy?"

"Let's go talk to Mrs. Blakely," Vanessa said, resigning herself to the fact that this man would be working with her. "We'll get the details worked out."

Vanessa called Bettina and arranged for her to meet them in the staff room. "So you found her, Shane," she said in her soft, lilting Caribbean accent as she sat down at the table with them. "I'm sorry I couldn't come down to the library with you, but that phone call was important." She shook her head and sighed. "There are some strange people in the world. Unfortunately, a lot of them are parents. Now, Shane," she went on, smiling at him. "Did Vanessa explain the ins and outs of the proposed program?"

"She did," Shane said with his easy smile. "I think it's a great idea."

"I thought he'd be good with Tommy," Vanessa put in. "You know—Tommy Hawkes, in Gail's room. I think he'd respond well to working with a man."

Bettina was nodding, one lean finger tapping the side of her mug. "Yes, Tommy would be just right." She grinned suddenly. "We'd be breaking you in easy, Shane. He's a good kid—he can even sit still for extended periods of time—five minutes at least!"

"Tell me about him," Shane urged, leaning forward on his elbows.

"Well," Bettina said, "he's eight years old. He spent most of his life in a remote mining community in the north of the province. After his father died in a mining accident last year his mother decided to move them to Winnipeg. It's been a pretty rough year for both of them, although I think things are beginning to improve."

Vanessa cut in. "But on top of everything else, Tommy's language skills are weak. We're not really sure why. We understand that no one ever read to him. And it's just the two of them at home. His brothers and sisters are grown, with families of their own. Anyway, we feel that he could really benefit from a regular reading program. The classroom teacher simply doesn't have the time to give him the individual attention he needs. This program should help him build up his vocabulary and gain a little confidence, too. And I hope it will give him encouragement to start reading on his own."

Shane was nodding, his eyes thoughtful. "If he lived up north for all those years, he'll probably like books on animals, the outdoors. I could start with some simple animal stories.''

Bettina looked at Vanessa and smiled, obviously pleased. ''Well, Shane, I have a feeling you're going to work out just fine.''

''I hope so. When would you like me to start?''

''Vanessa, the library's free on Tuesday and Thursday afternoons, isn't it? Those days would probably be the best—say, from one until two?''

''That'll be fine with me,'' Shane agreed. ''Will I be working in the library?''

''Yes. Vanessa will give you a hand—this program is her idea. Oh, there's Tommy's teacher now. Gail,'' she called. ''Can you spare a minute?'' The petite woman joined the small group. ''Gail Napier, meet Shane Wilder. He's volunteering for the new reading program. We'd like to start him working with Tommy.''

''Great,'' Gail said, sitting beside Shane, her big blue eyes looking curiously at him. ''Hey—I saw you interviewed on *The Journal* a couple of months ago. You write those Matt Savage books, don't you?''

Shane smiled. ''Yes, I do.''

''Oh, wow, that's great,'' Gail said. ''I just love reading them.''

''Thank you,'' Shane said, with a quick, smiling glance at Vanessa.

''I just love Matt. He's so adventurous, you know? A real man—he gets mixed up in the wildest things.'' Her eyes widened and she smiled at Shane.

Vanessa grimaced at the sound of Gail's breathless, little-girl's voice. She didn't care much for Gail and her constant, inane chatter. She wasn't stupid, Vanessa knew, but she could sure sound like it a lot of the time.

''Why don't you come up to my classroom, Shane,'' Gail suggested. ''I can show you some of Tommy's work so you can get an idea of what level he's at.''

Shane shook his head with a smile. "I'd rather start with a blank slate, if that's all right with you. That way I won't be prejudging him."

"Oh. Okay." Vanessa sensed obvious disappointment in Gail's eyes. "Well, if you do need any help, I'm in room—"

She was interrupted by the arrival of Carla, who slipped in between Shane and Vanessa on the other side of Gail. "Shane," she began right away. "I've been thinking—do you think you could come to my room some time and talk to the kids? They'd love to hear from a real live author."

"Oh, what a great idea," Gail said brightening. "Add me to your list, Shane."

"Whoa!" Bettina held up her hands. "Give the man a chance! You know how hard it is to get good volunteers—let's not scare him away."

"Maybe we can arrange something for later in the year," Shane said, flashing his wide, charming smile at both of them. "I plan on being around for a while."

Vanessa watched quietly. Oh, he was a flirt, all right. He was loving every minute of the attention Carla and Gail were giving him, encouraging them with his flashing dimples and laughing eyes. He looked at her suddenly and caught her troubled expression. He grinned and winked audaciously. With a little shake of her head, Vanessa smiled back in spite of herself.

As the bell to end recess sounded, Carla and Gail left, their reluctance plainly showing. Shane drained the last of his coffee and stood up.

"I should be off, too," he said. "Is there anything I should know?"

"If there is, it'll keep till Tuesday," Bettina said. "We'll see you then, unless you change your mind."

It was Vanessa's eyes he sought. "I won't change my mind," he said, his voice warm. "I promise." With an easy wave, he was gone.

"So that's Shane Wilder," Bettina said thoughtfully. "Think he'll do?"

"For Tommy—yes. But I think that he's going to cause quite a stir among some of the women around here."

Bettina looked at her closely. "How about you? Are you stirring?"

"I'm immune to worldly charm," Vanessa said mildly. "I had my fill of it with Todd."

"I think the man was interested, Van," Bettina persisted.

"He was interested in every female who walked through the door," Vanessa retorted.

Bettina laughed. "Maybe—but I saw the way he was looking at you. I think the interest might go a little deeper."

"I doubt it. Anyway, I'm not interested."

Bettina sighed and looked at her with an expression of concern for a long-suffering friend. "What kind of man *are* you interested in, Van? I found him quite delightful."

"I don't want delightful. I want solid and dependable."

"You don't have to marry the man. Just go out with him if he asks."

"I half expect he will." Vanessa laughed. "The question is—before or after Carla and Gail? And he hasn't even seen Shawna yet! The man's a flirt, Bettina."

"So go flirt a little. It'll do you good. You're too serious, Van. A lighthearted affair is probably just what you need in your life right now."

"I'm not looking for an affair." Vanessa frowned, shaking her head. "I want commitment."

"Since when did getting married become so important to you? I thought you had enough of that with Todd."

"I had enough of Todd, not marriage. I couldn't stay married to a man I didn't trust." She sighed. "I don't want to be married just to—to be married. I want a home and family. Oh, I know I have Gran and Marcie, but..." She looked at her friend and smiled. "I want what you've got, Bettina, with Ben and Haili. You know."

Bettina smiled softly. "Yeah. I know. And one day you'll find what you're looking for, Van. Well," she added, pushing her chair back from the table, "I've got to get back to work. A principal's paperwork is never done. Talk to you later."

Vanessa nodded and finished her tea before going back to the library. Would she ever have what Bettina had with Ben? Her own parents had had it, too; a relationship based on love and commitment, filled with an obvious joy and happiness. It wasn't too much to ask for herself, was it?

As she entered the library, she thought of Shane Wilder and her lips twitched with a reluctant smile. Delightful could be one of the words to describe him. Her smile widened and then became rueful. Disruptive was another. He was the type of man who would make his presence known.

Well, let him flash those dimples at the likes of Gail and Carla, Vanessa decided, sorting through a stack of books on the return cart. She wasn't interested.

CHAPTER TWO

VANESSA LET HERSELF IN through the kitchen door, smiling a cheerful greeting to her grandmother. "Hi, Gran."

Cora Evans looked up from the carrot she was paring. "Hello, dear. How was school today?"

"Great." A million mothers must be asking their children that same question right now, she mused. "Is Marcie home?"

"She's been doing her homework," Cora answered, inclining her head toward the kitchen table. "She's putting her books away so she can set the table."

Marcie Evans ran into the kitchen and stopped smack in front of Vanessa. "Hi, Aunt Van." She grinned, tucking a glossy, dark curl behind one ear. Fifteen years old, she had long, coltish limbs and sparkling hazel eyes.

"Hi, Marcie." Vanessa smiled warmly. "All finished with the homework?"

"Yeah. Except," she added making a face, "I've got to start a paper for English. Do you know what she wants us to do this time? We've got to write something about career choices people have made. And we've got to interview someone first." Marcie was obviously not pleased about the project. "I'd rather not."

Vanessa laughed. "You could make it easy on yourself and interview me. Or how about Bettina? She would be good. You could write about her background in the Caribbean."

"I suppose so. But Cory Switzer is doing his dad—he's a principal too, you know," she added, wiping the table and laying out place mats. "I think half the kids in the class are doing teachers. I want someone different."

"You'll think of something," Vanessa said.

"I hope so. If not, I guess I'll use you," Marcie said unenthusiastically, taking plates from the cupboard.

"Thanks for the vote of confidence, kid," Vanessa said dryly. Turning to her grandmother, she asked, "Is there anything I can do to help, Gran?"

"You go and change, Vanessa," Cora said, carefully grating the carrots into a bowl. "Then you can drain the rice."

"*Drain* the rice?"

"Yes, dear." Cora smiled. "I added too much water again, but it still tastes the same."

Vanessa shook her head and smiled fondly. "I don't know how you two would manage to eat if it wasn't for me." Vanessa kept the freezer well-stocked with ready-to-cook casseroles made on weekends.

"We can cook some meals pretty well," Marcie protested half-heartedly. "My bran muffins are good."

"Bran muffins are not a meal. Face it, Marcie," Vanessa teased. "You not only look like Gran, you inherited her cooking talents as well."

Cora chuckled. "That she did. And as bad as I am, I've improved since those first years I was married to John. I'm sure there were times when he wasn't sure what it was I set in front of him. But he never complained. Well," she amended, her hazel eyes twinkling, "not often, anyway."

"Maybe not," Vanessa said. "But he did learn to cook quite well in self-defense."

"He was a good man, your grandfather." Cora smiled softly in memory. "Go get changed now, Vanessa. Supper won't be long."

"Yes, Gran." Vanessa left the room smiling. She enjoyed the feeling of coming home so much. What would it be like arriving at an empty apartment each evening instead of the warm, happy home she shared with her grandmother and Marcie? Vanessa hung her coat in the hall closet and went upstairs.

She changed quickly into her favorite old jeans and an oversize sweatshirt. Standing in front of the mirror, she pulled out the pins holding up her hair and shook her head. Long golden hair, still streaked by the summer sun, fell around her shoulders in soft, ringletlike curls. Absently, she ran a comb through the curls. She was suddenly engulfed with unhappy thoughts from the past.

She could hardly believe ten years had passed since the accident that had left both her and Marcie orphans. Her large almond-shaped amber eyes grew troubled. She had been almost eighteen, Marcie, her brother David's child, barely five. David was driving home from a wedding with his wife, Lisa, and his parents. They never made it. A drunk driver sped through a red light, slamming head-on into their car. No one survived the flaming wreck.

Cora, devastated by the loss of her son and grandson, had taken Vanessa and Marcie into her home. The three of them had clung together, giving each other support until the pain gradually faded and they found themselves with a happy home of their own.

Todd Hughes had entered their little circle only briefly as it turned out. Vanessa had married him at nineteen and divorced him two years later. Immediately afterward she gave up the tiny apartment they'd shared and moved back into her grandmother's house.

Vanessa looked around her room with satisfaction. It had taken her ages to convert the long, low-cornered attic space into a comfortable living area. But the bright yet cozy living quarter was set up exactly to her liking. And, isolated from the rest of the house, it gave her the privacy she sometimes needed.

The built-in shelves along one wall were lined with her favorite books. A tiny, old-fashioned parlor stove stood on raised ceramic tiles opposite her state-of-the-art stereo system. Small plants lined the sills of the gable windows and a plush, cream-coloured carpet scattered with bright floral-patterned cushions covered the floor. The latest addition was a small whirlpool discretely set in a corner at the back of the room, enclosed by a Japanese silk screen she'd picked up at an antique market. It was a room she enjoyed and spent a lot of time in.

AFTER SUPPER, Vanessa settled in the living room with Cora and Marcie, the evening paper on her lap. Her grandmother sat opposite her in a comfortable armchair, a book held in her thin, wrinkled hands.

"Gran—have you read any books by Shane Wilder?"

Cora looked up from the page, blinking over top of her glasses. "Sure. He writes those detective novels, doesn't he, with— What's the name of the character?"

"Matt Savage," Vanessa filled in for her.

"Ah, yes." Cora nodded. "That's the one."

"What do you think of them?"

"They're quite good, actually—a combination of action and whodunit, with lots of convoluted clues. I'm usually kept guessing right to the end. His descriptions are great, too."

"Aren't they rather—well, geared toward men?" Vanessa asked.

"Not really. They're a bit short on romance for my liking—the hero gets a new woman in each book. But they're quite humorous in places, and never too—too... not masculine. What's the word?"

"Macho?" With a hero called Matt Savage, she would have thought that's exactly what they would be.

"By the way," Cora said, "did you know he lives in Winnipeg?"

"Um—yes, as a matter of fact, I did."

Something in Vanessa's voice made Cora look at her closely. "Have you met him?" she asked.

"Well, actually, he's volunteered for that reading program I've been wanting to start."

"Really? How exciting! What's he like?"

Vanessa shrugged. "He seemed all right, I suppose."

Cora sighed. "What I want to know, dear, is he anything like his hero, or is he a dried-up little man living vicariously through his writing?"

"I don't know anything about his hero, Gran, but he's far from being dried up, and," she added dryly, "I doubt that he does anything vicariously." He had the look of a man very much involved with life.

"Is he handsome?" Cora persisted.

"I suppose." Vanessa nodded remembering his strong face and the devilish glint in his clear gray eyes.

Marcie looked away from the television show she had been half following while listening to the conversation between her aunt and great-grandmother. "I've got a great idea," she said suddenly, sitting up straight in her chair, eyes sparkling. "I could interview Shane Wilder for my paper! You could ask him, couldn't you?" she asked Vanessa.

"I've hardly spoken to the man." Vanessa frowned in objection. "I don't think I should be asking for favors."

"But you'd do it for me, wouldn't you, Aunt Nessie?" Marcie pleaded. "It would be like a—a scoop for me. I'd probably get an A."

"You'll probably get an A anyway. You usually do."

"Aw, please, Aunt Nessie. Ask him—please?"

"Oh, no, not the Bambi eyes," Vanessa muttered to Cora as Marcie widened her eyes imploringly.

Cora looked up and laughed. "She gets you that way every time, Vanessa."

"Please?" Marcie requested, as if her young life depended upon Vanessa's answer.

Vanessa scowled. "Oh—I'll think about it."

Marcie knew her aunt well enough to know she would ask. "Thanks, Aunt Van. You're the greatest."

"I haven't said yes yet," she warned.

"But you will," Marcie said with confidence and a sweet smile.

Vanessa knew she would. What could the man say, except yes or no? If he did agree to it, she could arrange for Marcie to come to the school at Shane's convenience. If Marcie had all her questions ready beforehand, the interview wouldn't take up much of his time. Besides, she thought, staring absently at the newspaper in front of her, she couldn't deny that she was a bit curious about what he'd have to say if he agreed to do it. No doubt he was a very interesting man. Interesting—but dangerous? a warning voice asked. No, she thought, not to me. She could read men such as him like a book and was confident she could handle any little games he might want to play.

VANESSA INTRODUCED SHANE to Tommy and was pleased as he greeted the boy with a natural warmth. Tommy, slight and wiry, examined Shane cautiously through narrowed, pale-blue eyes before following him to a corner table in the back of the library.

They talked for a long time, though Tommy's end of the conversation was limited to brief nods or a shake of the head. As Shane began going through a picture book on Canadian animals, Tommy's restlessness was evident. But Shane turned the pages slowly, all the while talking to Tommy. His patience was admirable. Before long the redheaded child had taken an interest in the book. He was leaning closer, his curiosity unconsciously helping him overcome his shyness. Soon he was pointing to the pages, telling Shane about the animals he recognized.

Confident that things were going well between them, Vanessa turned her attention to the task she had started before lunch. Several boxes of new books had arrived and she was sorting through them, a job she loved. Included were brightly illustrated books, storybooks and information-type books, all crisp and clean and tempting. She leafed through many, pausing to read passages, putting some aside to read more thoroughly at a later time.

"Now I can see it."

Startled, Vanessa looked up from the page. Shane was standing in front of her desk. "See what?" she asked.

"You're sitting here, surrounded by books and totally absorbed in what you're reading." He smiled. "I can see why you're a librarian."

"Oh." Vanessa returned his smile a little self-consciously. "I do love books," she admitted. "I guess that's why I never feel like I've come to work when I walk in here every morning." She closed the book she had been reading and put it aside. "How did it go with Tommy? Are you through, already?"

"Yes. Pretty good, I think. I didn't want to just dive into the reading thing, so we spent most of the time talking. At least," he amended, "I talked. Tommy seemed to listen. He's a quiet little guy."

"He is," Vanessa agreed. "You have to realize that he spent most of his life in a remote area where he knew practically everyone. You can imagine the shock it must have been for him, moving to Winnipeg and seeing nothing but unfamiliar faces around him. And coming on top of his father's accident. Well, it's left him slightly withdrawn and a little bit wary of strangers. If you can be patient, I'm sure he'll come around."

"Oh, I can be very patient," Shane said, with a slow smile as he perched on the corner of her desk.

Vanessa ignored the intimation in his voice. "Does that patience extend to other aspects of your life like, say, interviews?" If she was going to ask, it might as well be now.

His eyes narrowed. "Sometimes," he said briefly. "Why?"

"Well, my niece, Marcie, would like to interview you. She's fifteen years old and very persuasive," Vanessa answered. "She's doing a paper on career choices and thinks yours is more interesting than mine. I know it's a lot to ask. And I hardly know—"

"I'll do it," he interrupted, then relaxed with a chuckle. "When?"

"You will? Great. Marcie will be thrilled. I thought next week, after one of your sessions with Tommy. She can come here, and if she has all her questions ready, it shouldn't take too long—and she'll still have a couple of days to write it up."

"I have a better idea. Let's all meet at your place and do it there."

Vanessa looked at him suspiciously. "Why?" she asked bluntly.

His smile was quick and charming. "To make it easier for your niece, of course. How about tonight?"

She hesitated, feeling reluctant to have him in the privacy of her home. But it would be more convenient for Marcie, and she knew Cora would be thrilled. "All right," she said finally.

She scribbled her address on a piece of paper and handed it to him. "Eight o'clock?"

"Eight o'clock," he agreed. "See you then." He picked up his jacket and left.

"How did it go with Shane and Tommy?" Bettina asked later that afternoon.

"Good, I think," Vanessa answered. "He took the time to talk to Tommy—and Tommy was talking back by the time the hour was up. I think it's going to work out."

"Uh-huh. And how did you get along with him?"

"Oh—all right," Vanessa said. "He's coming over to the house tonight," she added casually.

Bettina grinned delightedly. "Hey—that's fast work. On your part or his?"

"Marcie's." Vanessa laughed. "She has to do a paper on someone with an interesting career for English class. She picked him over you or me."

"Smart girl." Bettina chuckled. "And he agreed to be interviewed?"

"Quite easily, actually. I was surprised."

"Could it be he's hoping to score some points with the aunt?"

"Bettina—I honestly don't think he's as interested as all that," Vanessa protested. "And even if he is—well, I'm not."

"Well, I happen to think he's interested, and you should be, too," Bettina said assuredly, ignoring her friend's scowl of objection as she pushed back her chair and stood to leave. "Anyway, fill me in on the details tomorrow."

THE DOORBELL RANG just after eight. Vanessa stood up quickly, smoothing back her hair and straightening her skirt. "Wait here, Marcie," she said.

She answered the front door, smiling a polite greeting at Shane. Standing aside, she let him enter.

"This is a very nice place you have," he said, bringing in the fragrance of a drizzly autumn night. He shook the moisture from his dark curls and handed her his jacket. "Far too big for one person," he added, looking around the spacious hall with its winding staircase of polished oak.

"There are three of us," Vanessa said, hanging his jacket in the closet.

"Three of you?" There was a look of dismay on his face.

Vanessa had to laugh as she shook her head. "Relax. I've got a grandmother and a niece. This is our place. Come on in and meet them."

"Oh. Good. You had me worried for a minute there," he admitted, his eyes laughing lazily into hers. "I thought maybe you were married."

"No." Not anymore, Vanessa thought, somehow uncomfortable that he'd raised the subject.

They entered the living room and Shane instantly charmed both Marcie and Cora. "Mrs. Evans," he said, taking Cora's hand gently in his, "I can see where Marcie gets her prettiness."

Cora beamed. "Why, thank you, Mr. Wilder. It's been a long time since anyone bothered to try and flatter me."

"Oh, yeah?" Marcie grinned. "What about old Mr. Aitkens down at the senior's center?"

"Someone young, dear," Cora joked with a pleased smile at Shane. "I'd like to tell you, Mr. Wilder, how much I enjoy your books, especially the later ones."

"Thank you, Mrs. Evans. That's always nice to hear. But please—call me Shane."

"I will, if you'll call me Cora. Now, Shane, may I get you something to drink?"

"I wouldn't mind a cup of coffee, if it isn't too much trouble."

"It's no trouble at all. Can you give me a hand, Vanessa? Marcie, do you have your questions ready?"

"Yes, Gran. I'll wait until you get back with the coffee, though. You don't mind if they stay for the interview, do you—Shane?" Marcie sneaked his first name in with a quick glance at Vanessa, who ignored it. Obviously it didn't bother him.

"Make yourself comfortable," Vanessa said, gesturing to a big, overstuffed armchair. "We'll be back in a minute." She followed Cora into the kitchen.

"You know," Cora said as the kitchen door swung shut behind them, "he looks just like I always pictured Matt Savage." She took a tray from the cupboard. "And he's such a charming, handsome man. Don't you agree, dear?"

"Yes, Gran," Vanessa admitted. There was no denying it. She poured boiling water over freshly ground coffee while Cora organized the tray with cups, cream, sugar and an assortment of homemade cookies.

"I'm glad Marcie doesn't mind us sitting in on her interview," Cora went on. "I find myself very interested in what he might say."

Vanessa set the pot of coffee down. She was just as curious as Cora, she confessed, picking up the tray and carrying it into the living room.

Marcie started her questions after the coffee had been poured. "What made you decide to become a writer?" she asked.

"It wasn't really something I decided to do," Shane acknowledged, holding a cup of coffee in his long, lean fingers. "At least not at first. It grew from a university assignment." He smiled at Marcie's look of surprise. "I was actually majoring in economics," he went on, "but had signed up for a class in creative writing. Mainly," he added with a chuckle, "because I saw someone in the enrollment line I wanted to meet." He caught the flash of derision in Vanessa's eyes and grinned at her.

"Anyway, the professor wanted each of us to pick one of the popular genres of fiction—sci-fi, westerns, romance— and write three or four chapters and a synopsis of our own story. I liked mysteries, so I invented Matt Savage and involved him in *The Case of the Purloined Pearls*. It started out quite tongue-in-cheek. I wasn't that serious about it at all, figuring I'd be lucky to get a pass out of the course." He paused to smile at Marcie, her head bent, as she scribbled furiously in the notebook balanced on her lap.

"Then what?" she asked looking up.

"I surprised myself," Shane admitted. "The writing came easily and I became intrigued with the whole process, and enjoyed working out clues that would leave the reader guessing. I found out there was a lot more to Matt Savage than I'd ever intended."

"So is he, like, your alter ego?" Marcie asked, looking pleased with the question.

"I suppose parts of Matt are me," Shane said. "And of course, there is a part of me that would like some of the action and excitement of Matt's life—what man wouldn't? But basically he's just a product of my imagination, the type of larger-than-life hero people expect in a mystery novel."

Marcie nodded. "Okay, so what happened after you turned it in?"

He grinned. "I passed. And my prof was encouraging; he thought I should pursue writing, but—" he shrugged "—I wasn't all that interested at that point."

"What made you change your mind?"

"My friend—the one I met in the line," he added with a quick, teasing wink at Vanessa, "sent what I had written to a publisher. They were interested and dangled a contract along with a nice advance in front of me. What poor, struggling university student could resist? I started writing between classes and studying, and managed to finish that first book. It did well and they wanted more."

"Were you able to make a living at it right away?"

"No, not really. While I was in university, I managed about as well as I would have working part-time and during the summer. After I graduated, I decided to pursue writing. I had to take all kinds of part-time and temporary jobs to support myself at first. It wasn't exactly what I had planned, but I found writing gave me a freedom I would never have had with a regular career."

Marcie nodded. "And more money, probably," she said guilelessly.

There was a hint of indulgence in Shane's smile. "Eventually," he agreed.

"I wanted to read some of your books before I interviewed you," Marcie said, tucking a strand of glossy dark hair behind one ear. "But I didn't get a chance. I sort of skimmed through a few chapters of one—*Double or Nothing*. I kind of like it, even though there isn't much romance and stuff."

Shane chuckled. "Romance being better suited to a girl your age than the exploits of Matt Savage."

"Yeah, well, maybe," Marcie agreed. "But I like mysteries and stuff, too. Aunt Vanessa likes me to read all kinds of books. She says books let us experience different things, maybe even keep us from making mistakes in real life." Marcie grinned suddenly, her hazel eyes twinkling. "Maybe she should have read more love stories before she ma—"

"Marcie." Vanessa cut quickly into her niece's near art-less disclosure. "Maybe Mr. Wilder would like some more coffee."

"Oh." Marcie looked at her a little guiltily. She had not missed the warning note in her aunt's voice. "Would you—uh, Mr. Wilder?" she asked, not daring to use his first name again in front of her aunt.

"Please," he said, holding out his cup. "And Marcie, call me Shane. Everyone does. Any more questions?" he asked, after she had refilled his cup.

"Just a few," Marcie answered, settling back down with her pen and notepad. "About publication and stuff like that."

Vanessa hardly listened to the last few questions. She had seen the way Shane's eyes had darted curiously to her after she had interrupted Marcie, before Marcie could say anything about Todd. Vanessa hoped he wouldn't ask about it later. It wasn't something she liked to talk about, and she would feel especially vulnerable under the gleam of Shane's too-knowing eyes.

"Well, Shane," Cora said when Marcie had finished, "I certainly enjoyed listening in on this interview. It was very nice of you to consent to it."

"Yes, it was," Marcie agreed quickly. "Thank you very much, Shane. I really appreciate it. I'm sure it's good for an A. In fact, if it's okay, I think I'll go get started writing it up now, while it's still fresh in my mind. And," she added with a grin, "I'd like to finish *Double or Nothing*, even if Matt doesn't keep the girl in the end." She stood up, gathering her papers together. "Good night, Shane. And thanks again."

"You're welcome, Marcie," Shane said warmly. "I enjoyed it. Let me know how you make out."

"Sure. Will do."

"Help me take these things back to the kitchen before you go up," Cora said, putting the cups on the tray.

"Sure, Gran." Marcie took the tray and followed Cora into the kitchen. "Night, Shane, Aunt Nessie," she called over her shoulder.

"Nessie?" Shane murmured, his eyebrows rising.

"For her use only," Vanessa said quickly. "No one else would dare."

"What would happen if someone did?" he asked, his eyes gleaming.

Vanessa smoothed her skirts over her knees. "I'd deck them," she said calmly.

Shane let out a shout of laughter. "I would have thought you were too ladylike for fisticuffs."

"I am. Except under provocation."

"And—Nessie is provocation?"

"Most definitely."

"What else provokes you?" he asked, leaning forward.

"Bullies, liars and cheats," she answered promptly.

"Ah, of course." He nodded. "If I told you I'm none of the above, would you go out with me?"

"Go out as in to step outside to say good night when you leave?" she asked, deliberately obtuse.

"No, silly lady. I mean go out as in on a date—to dinner, a show, roller skating, a walk in the park . . . Will you?"

Vanessa gave a little smile as she shook her head. "No."

His eyes widened in surprise. "No?" he repeated. "Why not?"

"I just don't think it would be a good idea." She looked at her hands clasped on her lap. I don't play your kind of games, she added to herself.

"Why not?" he asked again. "Are you engaged or involved with someone?"

For a moment she was tempted to lie. "No," she said slowly, glancing at him.

"But you still won't go out with me." His tone was so plaintive that she had to smile.

"No, I won't. But thanks for asking."

"I'll ask again," he said, surprised but not put off. "Just in case you change your mind." His look said clearly that he was sure she would. "In the meantime, I've got to run."

"A date?" Vanessa murmured as he stood up.

"No," he said over his shoulder as he went into the hall. "A walk in the rain, all by myself. It's a beautiful night," he added as he took his jacket from her. "The rain is soft and misty, and there's that wonderful smell of autumn in the air. I even heard a flock of geese flying high over the city as I came in." He zipped his jacket and cocked his head to one side, his eyes warm as they held hers. "It's far too romantic to go it alone," he said softly. "Aren't you tempted?"

A part of her was, but she pushed it aside. "I hate getting wet. Enjoy yourself," she added, opening the door for him.

"I will," he said, with a chuckle. "Say good-night and thanks to Cora for me. I don't want to bother her. And Vanessa..."

She looked at him cautiously. "Yes?"

"I don't give up easily," he murmured, laying a finger briefly across her lips. "Not when it's something I really want." He turned with a wave. "See you Thursday."

Vanessa watched him run easily down the steps and disappear into the night. Shaking her head ruefully, she shut the door and rubbed a knuckle over her lips, still feeling his fleeting touch and wondering just how persistent he might be—and just how much resistance she really had when it came to smooth-talking, charmingly handsome men. Her track record wasn't all that good.

"Is he gone?" Cora asked, poking her head around the kitchen doorway.

"Yes—he said to say good-night and thanks. And Gran, you didn't have to hide yourself in the kitchen. There was nothing personal about his visit."

"Maybe not, dear," Cora said. "But I wanted to give him a chance. He's a very nice young man. Handsome, too— something like your grandfather was. Did he ask you out?"

"Yes, he did."

"And?" Cora prompted.

"There is no and. I turned him down."

Cora frowned. "Why? You should have jumped at the chance."

"He's not my type, Gran."

"Nonsense. He's any woman's type. What's the problem?"

Vanessa sighed, wishing Cora would let it drop. "There is no problem. I just didn't want to go out with him."

Cora shook her head. "Well, I think you're being foolish. The man was obviously interested."

"Gran, he was just as obviously interested in half the female staff at school. What am I supposed to do—get in line?"

"Push your way to the front, dear," Cora said with a cheerful smile. "Maybe you'd stay there for a while."

"I don't want a while, Gran. I want forever. I've got a feeling Shane is a lot like Todd as far as women are concerned. The more the merrier. I've smartened up too much to get caught by a man like that again." She frowned suddenly and shook her head, puzzled. "A good-looking man comes on the scene and suddenly everyone is advising me to throw myself at him, have an affair. Even *you*, Gran! What is it with everyone all of a sudden?"

"If by everyone you mean Bettina, it's because we're worried about you," Cora said. "You've become far too serious over the last couple of years. You need to loosen up, Vanessa, before you no longer can." She sighed and shook her head. "When was the last time you had a date—a real date?"

Vanessa frowned. "I can't be bothered anymore—getting all dressed up to go sit through dinner with a man I hardly know, trying to make polite conversation all evening, all the while knowing that he's wondering if he'll be able to get me into his bed later. It all seems so pointless. I wish it could be fun, exciting, like it used to be. But it isn't."

"Shane Wilder would be fun," Cora persisted.

"But his intentions wouldn't be serious." Vanessa said with conviction. "I'm looking for more than a few laughs, Gran. I know what I want, what I need from a man, and I'm not going to settle for anything less."

"And so you shouldn't. But you've got to put a little effort into finding Mr. Right—he isn't going to waltz through the door and sweep you off your feet." Cora sighed and squeezed Vanessa's arm gently. "You've closed up so much since Todd. I worry about you, about how alone you're going to be when I'm gone and Marcie's grown. Open up a bit, dear. Let life back into your heart."

Vanessa hugged her grandmother close. "You don't need to worry about me, Gran. Basically, I like my life, and I'll be okay whether I'm alone or not." She kissed a soft, crepey cheek. "Now, would you like me to make you some cocoa before you go up to bed?"

After sharing a cup of cocoa with Cora and saying goodnight, Vanessa looked in on Marcie. The girl was in bed reading, halfway through Shane's book.

"Hi, kid," Vanessa said, coming into the room. "Did you get the interview written up?"

Marcie looked up from the book. "No, but I've got it all organized. It shouldn't take long to finish."

"Good. And Marcie, I thought you handled yourself very well. You asked some good questions."

"Thanks, Aunt Van. And...listen, I'm sorry about what I was going to say about you and Uncle Todd. I was out of line. I guess it wasn't any of his business, was it?"

"No, but don't worry about it. And you know, sweetie," she added, "I'm not really afraid you'll make the same mistakes I did. You're a much more sensible girl than I was at your age."

Marcie looked down, folding the edge of the bedspread between her fingers. "Yeah, well—I'll never get married anyway."

"Never?" Vanessa asked.

Marcie shrugged, her narrow shoulders rising under the covers. "I doubt it. I mean, it's not very realistic, is it? Half the kids I know have divorced parents—some of them more than once. And the other half complain about how their parents are always fighting. Then there's you and Uncle Todd. I don't think marriage works in real life."

Vanessa sat on the edge of Marcie's bed, concerned at the skepticism she could hear in the young girl's voice. "Marcie, I don't want you to judge marriage by what happened between Todd and me. Marriage can be a wonderful thing with the right person. Your parents were happy together—so were mine, and Gran and Grampa. It can and does work for a lot of people."

"Yeah, I suppose." Marcie looked wary.

"If you have any doubts, look at Ben and Bettina—and, believe me, they aren't an exception. The main thing," she added, "is not to be in a rush, to wait for the right man. That was my mistake with Todd. We weren't meant for each other, and I didn't take the time to find that out. Okay?"

"Sure." She grinned and tapped a finger on the cover of Shane's book. "Maybe I'll be a female Matt Savage and have lots of men in my life instead of settling for just one."

Vanessa shook her head with a smile, seeing the teasing light in Marcie's eyes. "You'd better not, kiddo," she said in light warning, patting Marcie's knee as she stood up. "Better get some sleep now."

"I'll just finish this chapter," Marcie said, opening the book again. "I kind of like it." She snuggled under the covers and grinned. "I kind of like *him*! Night, Aunt Nessie."

"Good night, Marcie," Vanessa said, giving her a quick kiss on the cheek. "See you in the morning."

Vanessa went up the narrow stairs to her own room, perturbed about the doubts Marcie had toward marriage. Vanessa had always tried to set a good example for her niece to follow, but had obviously failed miserably as far as giving her a positive look at married life. Marcie had been fond of

Todd, and the divorce had hurt her. Vanessa hoped the experience hadn't turned Marcie off marriage, but would make her extracareful about the man she decided to spend her life with.

Not like I was, Vanessa reflected as she got out of her clothes and turned on the water to fill the tub. After adding a splash of fragrant bubble bath, she slid into the steamy water with a sigh of pleasure.

She had a serious, somewhat shy nature, which kept her withdrawn and awkward around the opposite sex. Except for a few rather unsuccessful dates during high school, she'd had relatively little to do with boys. Todd had been her first real boyfriend.

She had met him halfway through her second year of university. Just beginning to recover from the horrendous shock of the accident, she had been instantly attracted to his good looks and charming manner. Having a structured existence herself, she found that his carefree life-style appealed to her. Todd seemed all fun, laughter and good times. Starry-eyed, she'd fallen deeply in love almost instantly, feeling a thrilling sense of wonder that such a popular, handsome man would want her. Six months after they had met, they were married.

The first year of their marriage had seemed wonderful, although in retrospect Vanessa realized there had been problems she refused to see. Todd's charm and high spirits weren't reserved for her alone. There always seemed to be some woman who made it obvious that she found Todd attractive and, to Vanessa's dismay, he never seemed averse to joining in the flirtation. But Vanessa convinced herself it was all just a harmless bit of fun—party games, she told herself. She loved her husband. She trusted him.

Vanessa slid a little farther down in the tub and stirred the delicate bubbles with her fingers, her eyes narrow with memories.

She had started teaching during their second year of marriage while Todd continued at university. Soon she had little time for parties and socializing. Serious about her chosen career, she worked hard preparing lessons and marking papers, often remaining in her classroom long after everyone else had left for the day.

Knowing Todd's restlessness, his need for physical activity, she had been understanding when he began to spend more time away from home, playing handball or hockey with his friends. If he came home late, she'd convince herself it was because he'd stopped for a couple of drinks after the game.

She tried not to mind when he started going to an occasional party without her. It was a struggle not to be clinging and jealous, to shut out pictures of the women she knew he would laugh and dance with, but she had work to do and she desperately wanted to prove herself to be an understanding wife. It's different for him, she'd told herself. He's still a student and should be more involved in the university's social activities.

"There's a party tonight," he'd said to her one morning before she left for work. "I don't suppose you can make it."

"No," she answered, running a comb through her hair. "I've got those parent-teacher interviews, remember?" She sighed. "My first ones—I'll be a nervous wreck by the time they day's over. But you go ahead if you want," she added, wishing he wouldn't, wishing he'd be home for her when she finished.

Todd put his arms around her, kissing the top of her head. "I probably will. Thanks, hon."

Vanessa pushed down a feeling of disappointment and leaned against him. "Who's having the party?"

"Uh—Rochelle. We were at her place last summer for a barbecue. You remember?"

Vanessa nodded, remembering Rochelle, a shapely law student with long dark hair and a pretty face. Closing her eyes for a moment, she controlled an unwarranted rush of jealousy. She turned in his arms and smiled at him with the trust he deserved. "Have fun," she said, and added with a

murmur, "if I'm asleep when you get home—wake me up."
She kissed him softly.

The interviews had gone much more smoothly than she'd
thought possible. Excited by a feeling of success, she decided on the spur of the moment to join Todd at the party.
Rochelle, she recalled, rented a tiny house near the university. Vanessa parked her car in front and went to the door,
hoping she could persuade Todd to leave early. She really
wanted to be alone with him. Expecting loud music and a
babble of voices within, she didn't bother to knock. Pushing open the door, she walked directly into the living room.

There was a party all right, a private party for two. Amid
flickering candlelight and empty wine bottles, Vanessa
found her husband in the arms of another woman. With a
low moan of pain, she fled home, knowing she would never
forget the shock, the utter humiliation of that moment.

It was much later when Todd finally crept home. She had
calmed down enough to try to listen to what he had to say,
hoping something would erase the vivid, sickening pictures
from her mind.

"It's you I love, Vanessa," he said. "Rochelle—well,
she's no big deal."

Vanessa shook her head in bewilderment. "Then—why?"

In spite of his contrite, sheepish look, a touch of hateful
smugness colored his voice. "She just kept after me," he
said, and shrugged. "I guess she caught me in a moment of
weakness. Forgive me, Van?" he pleaded.

But Vanessa had looked into his shifting blue eyes and
had known, as sure as if he'd told her, that it had happened
before and would happen again. When confronted, he'd
scarcely bothered to deny it. For Todd, sex was a mere
physical act, one he was able to separate easily from the love
he felt for her. In his mind, he really hadn't done anything
wrong—except get caught.

Vanessa knew she could never trust him again. Their
marriage was over.

Sitting up in the tub, she reached for a sponge and rubbed it idly over her arms. She had seen Todd several times since the divorce—it was inevitable, with both of them working in the same school division—but she had felt no pangs of stubborn love. What she'd felt for him had gone, destroyed by his betrayal, and she gradually came to realize that if she'd been a little older and wiser, she would never have married him. The guilt she had for a failed marriage soon disappeared as she understood it could never have worked. Todd just wasn't able to commit himself to one woman.

Vanessa watched the water drain from the tub then lifted herself out, reaching for the large, fluffy towel on the wicker stool beside her. It could have been worse, she thought. It could have been years before she'd found out Todd's true nature, and by then there might have been children to consider.

Children. Vanessa sighed softly. In a way, she wished there had been a child. She wanted children so badly sometimes it was like an ache. Would she ever have any? Biologically, time was beginning to run out, but before she could even think of having children, she had to find a man who would love her as she yearned to be loved, someone she could trust to make a secure loving home with her.

She turned out the lights and slid into bed, the soft, warm comfort of the water-filled mattress folding around her. Surely there was someone out there for her. She wasn't asking for the impossible, was she?

CHAPTER THREE

VANESSA HAD A FEW MINUTES alone with Tommy before Shane was due to arrive.

"Well, Tommy," she said, sitting beside him at the table. "Are you looking forward to working with Mr. Wilder?"

Tommy nodded vigorously, then carefully unfolded a grubby sheet of paper. "I got some pictures I drew to show him."

Vanessa smoothed the paper and looked at the smudged drawings. "These are very good, Tommy," she said with an affectionate smile. "I like the way you draw animals."

Tommy ducked his head, shyly pleased. "Today, we're gonna look at some more aminal books."

"Animal books," Vanessa said, correcting him gently. "Yes, I know. I picked out some that I thought you might enjoy. One is about a hawk—like your name." She pulled the book from the small pile on the table and handed it to him. "Why don't you look at it while you're waiting for Mr. Wilder?"

While Tommy busied himself with the book, Vanessa began piling old magazines on a table on the other side of the room, then fetched scissors, glue and several sheets of manila paper. By the time Shane had arrived, she was already engaged in her afternoon task. Shane caught her eye and smiled a greeting before sitting down with Tommy.

Vanessa had deliberately set herself up to get a clear view of the two of them. She told herself it was merely to observe how Tommy was reacting, but she found herself watching Shane with undeniable appreciation. He was so natural with the boy. His shoulders looked so broad and athletic under his blue V-necked sweater. She liked the way his dimples quivered in the corners of his mouth awaiting his smile. And he smiled often, fondly, at Tommy, who responded with an eagerness that made Vanessa confident the partnership would work.

As she snipped away at the magazines, she found herself wondering what a date with Shane would be like. He would be fun, she thought with a little smile, and demandingly passionate. He had an aura of sensuality, she realized suddenly, looking up with narrowed, speculative eyes. It was evident in his laughing, well-shaped mouth and in the lean, masculine grace of his body. He would be a good lover, she knew as a wave of unexpected, unwanted longing washed through her.

With a frown of consternation, she dropped her eyes to the table, hating to acknowledge that she found him attractive. Sex without love and commitment was not for her, and she was certain that was all that a relationship with a man like Shane would offer. She sneaked another look across the room and shook her head slightly, admitting reluctantly to herself that, no matter how strong her convictions, Shane Wilder could prove to be a very tempting man.

At the end of the hour, Shane said goodbye to a beaming Tommy and made his way to Vanessa.

"Hi," he said, sitting across from her, his smile quick and warm.

"Hi." She smiled back. "How did it go?"

"Great—he showed a lot of interest in the books," Shane answered, looking pleased. "I think we're going to make a good team. I like Tommy."

"And Tommy likes you. That's half the battle right there—he'll want to please you."

"I think I'll read him a proper story next time—an animal adventure, I think."

"I'll pick out a few for you," Vanessa promised. "Then he can choose the one he wants to hear."

"Thanks." Shane rested his elbows on the table and leaned forward, gray eyes gleaming as they rested on her. "You look like you belong in a kindergarten class today. What's with the cutouts?"

"I'm working on the picture file," she said, looking away from his bright eyes. "The teachers often want pictures of animals, birds, insects—anything that might help to illustrate their lessons. I glue the pictures to the manila and label them before putting them in that file cabinet over there," she added, gesturing across the room.

"Can I help?"

Vanessa looked at him, a hint of dismay in her green-gold eyes. "I'm sure you have other things to do."

"No. Besides, it looks like fun." He grinned. "What's the matter—don't you want me?"

Vanessa ignored the suggestive quirk of his eyebrows and handed him the scissors. "You cut, I'll paste," she ordered. She wasn't going to argue with him. She hoped he'd grow bored and leave before long.

"Yes, ma'am," he said, taking the scissors and snipping them in the air. "What do I cut?"

"Anything that looks interesting. Animals and birds, any kind of industry, pictures of people in different cultures . . . that kind of thing."

Time passed quickly. Shane was circumspect enough should any student come into the library looking for a book or wanting information, but when they were alone, his outrageous comments kept her laughing. She found it impossible to keep herself cool and distant and, to her dismay, she found her attraction to him growing at an alarming pace.

Bettina came in just before the recess bell. "Shane—hello. I see she's kept you working overtime."

Shane nodded and managed to look morose. "A real slave driver, this one. Those big, soft eyes had me fooled."

Bettina laughed. "She can make it up to you by taking you to coffee. I came to tell you, Vanessa, that someone brought in a big box of doughnuts. First come gets best pick. See you in the staff room?"

"In a couple of minutes," Vanessa said, carefully laying a picture of a family of raccoons on a sheet of manila. "Save me a chocolate-glazed?"

"And a jam buster for me," Shane said, gathering up scraps for the wastepaper basket.

"Will do. Don't be too long, though," she cautioned as she left the room. "I can't keep a hoard of hungry teachers at bay for long."

Shane sat back in his chair and watched her leave, his eyes appreciative of her graceful, swaying walk. "That woman," he said with a gleam in his eyes, "is stunning."

"She's married," Vanessa said shortly. "Happily married."

"Really?" There was a note of cynical disbelief in his voice. "Isn't that a contradiction in terms?" He looked at her disapproving expression and added, "Don't worry. I never date married women—even if most of them would be willing."

Vanessa was frowning. "How do you know they're willing?"

He gave a derisive snort. "It's in the eyes, sweetie. It gives them away every time." He stood up and stretched lithely. "Let's go get that coffee. I could use a cup."

"You go ahead," Vanessa said. "I'll be along in a minute." She slowly straightened up the table, disturbed by his cynicism toward marriage. She put the supplies away and went to get her purse, wondering just what his problem was.

She stood in the doorway to the staff room for a moment. Shane was seated across the table from Bettina and flanked by Carla and Gail, each laughingly responsive to his flirtatious behavior. As Vanessa went to sit in the chair Bettina had saved for her, she felt a pang of disappointment. She had to admit that it would have been nice if Shane was attracted to her and didn't just give her attention because she was a woman, part of the game he so obviously enjoyed playing. He had asked her out and she had refused. Who would he turn his interest to now?

She spent her coffee break listening to Gail and Carla chatter like a couple of magpies, each vying for Shane's attention. Shane enjoyed every minute of it. Vanessa caught Bettina's eye and raised her eyebrows. See? her expression said. Bettina merely grinned and closed one dark eye in a wink.

"By the way, Shane," Bettina broke into the conversation. "My husband and I are giving a Halloween party Saturday night for the staff. As the newest member of that staff will you come? We'd love to have you."

"Oh, yes," Gail said enthusiastically. "We'll have a panic!"

"Wear a costume," Carla instructed, leaning toward Shane so that her arm brushed against his. "There'll be prizes for the best."

"Coffee mugs and gag gifts," Bettina said. "A bottle of wine if you're lucky."

"How can I resist?" Shane grinned. "I'd love to come, Bettina."

"Good. Vanessa will give you the details and directions to my place." She stood up as the bell went. "And Shane— be prepared. My husband, Ben, will undoubtedly haul out all of his copies of your books to be autographed." With a wave, she left, followed by a reluctant Gail and Carla as students began to stream through the hall toward their classrooms.

As the staff room emptied, Vanessa scribbled Bettina's address on a paper napkin and pushed it across the table. "Here's the address," she told Shane. "It's just off Academy. Things will get started around eight."

"How about I pick you up?" Shane asked hopefully, tucking the napkin into his shirt pocket.

Vanessa shook her head quickly. "No, thank you. I'll be leaving early to help Bettina get things set up."

Shane's lips quirked in resignation. "Okay. But tell me—what kind of costume are you wearing?"

"I'm not sure yet," Vanessa answered. "I'm still thinking about it."

"I've got some ideas," he said.

"I'll bet you do," she said dryly.

"How about I'll go as an Arabian sheikh and you can come as my harem," he said.

Vanessa shook her head, smiling. "No, Shane."

"Me Tarzan, you Jane?"

Vanessa burst out laughing. "Let you loose dressed in nothing but a loincloth? I don't think so."

"It was the idea of you with your hair down, dressed in a few strategically placed tiger stripes, that appealed to me," he said, his dimples playing in his cheeks. "Is it long?"

She blinked. "Is what long?"

"Your hair," he said. "Is it long?"

"Um—yes, it is. Quite." She touched the sides self-consciously.

"Wear it loose on Saturday night," he urged, his voice low as he leaned across the table. "I'd love to see it flowing around your shoulders."

She looked quickly away from the warm, desiring look in his eyes, feeling an answering flutter deep inside. "I have to get back to the library," she said, hastily pushing back her chair. "Thank you for your help this afternoon."

"Anytime," Shane said. "See you Saturday night."

"YOU COULD TRY to look a little more glamorous," Marcie complained mildly. She was lying on Vanessa's bed watching her get ready for the party.

"I think she's gonna look neat," piped up Haili, Bettina's twelve-year-old daugher, who was spending the night with Marcie and Cora.

"Thank you, Haili," Vanessa said. "Halloween is supposed to be spooky and gruesome, Marcie. I'll save the glamour for some other night."

She sat in front of the mirror, scraping her hair back and fastening it tightly to her scalp, reminded of Shane's request that she wear it down. Under the interested eyes of the two girls, she finished smoothing on a pale, whitish make-up base, then carefully outlined her eyes with a dark liner, smudging it slightly. She did her lips with a dark red lipstick.

"Okay, girls," she said. "Look the other way for a minute."

Marcie and Haili squirmed around on the bed until they were facing the other direction. "What are you doing?" Haili asked.

"Putting on the finishing touches," Vanessa explained. "Be patient for a moment."

She slipped into a body-hugging, floor-length black dress with wide, flowing sleeves. It was an old dress, something she had picked up at a rummage sale, but it suited her and accentuated the natural curve of her hips and the swell of her small, round breasts. Reaching into a shopping bag, she pulled out a wig, shaking out the long, black nylon strands before pulling it on. With a lipstick brush, she added a glistening scarlet drop to the corner of her mouth and then pushed a pair of plastic fangs over her teeth.

"Count to ten and then turn around," she said, standing up and striking a pose.

"...nine, ten!" shouted Haili as she turned around. Her brown eyes widened. "Ever neat!" she exclaimed. "A vampire!"

"Hey—you look great," Marcie said. "Sort of spooky and glamorous. You hardly look like you."

"Good." Vanessa laughed, taking a final look in the mirror. The overall effect was good, she thought, pleased. With the black wig and smudged-looking eyes, she would hardly be recognizable. "Well," she said, glancing at the clock on her bedside table, "it's time to go."

"Can we stay up here, Aunt Van?" Marcie asked. "We'd like to listen to some music."

"Just make sure it isn't too loud for Gran, and remember to turn everything off when you go down."

"Okay. Thanks."

Vanessa left the two of them rooting through her music collection in search of something they didn't consider too antiquated. In spite of the age difference, Haili and Marcie enjoyed each other's company. In fact, Bettina and Haili, along with Ben, seemed as much family as they did friends. It was a relationship they all enjoyed.

"Well, Gran?" Vanessa asked, standing in the doorway to the living room.

Cora looked up from her book. "Very nice," she approved. "I like that drop of blood. It's quite effective. Are you leaving now?"

"As soon as the cab gets here. Oh—I left some money with Marcie. They want to order a pizza later on. They're in my room right now, listening to music. Don't let them drive you crazy, okay?"

"I can still crack the whip if necessary," Cora said mildly. The cab pulled up outside the house. "There's your ride, dear. Have a good time."

"I shouldn't be back too late," Vanessa said. "Good night, Gran. I'll tell you all about it tomorrow."

"VANESSA?" Ben answered the door, looking askance at her disguise.

"It's me," Vanessa said, showing her plastic fangs in a smile. "Nice costume, Ben," she said as she stepped inside and removed her coat. The Viking costume, complete with horned helmet, suited his tall, broad build and thick, reddish-blond beard.

"Bettina picked it out," Ben said, hanging her coat in the hall closet. "And speaking of costumes, yours is pretty good. I hardly recognized you."

Bettina came through from the kitchen dressed in a colorful African costume, beaded headdress swinging around the graceful curve of her chin. She made a startling contrast to her husband's rugged blondness.

"I thought you said you had his-and-her costumes," Vanessa said, admiring Bettina's outfit.

"They are," Bettina said with a mischievous wink. "Later the seafaring Viking gets to plunder the African village."

Vanessa chuckled. "Right."

"I like your costume," Bettina went on. "Especially the fangs. You look slinky but spooky." She grinned. "Who are you going to vamp tonight?"

Vanessa gave a little groan and shook her head. "Who is there? Just the usual group..."

"Seems to me there will be some—ah, new blood tonight," Bettina said, grinning. "A certain handsome volunteer, if I remember correctly."

Vanessa made a face and changed the subject. "Let's get in that kitchen and get things ready before everyone gets here."

They laid out the party foods on trays and platters, handing them to Ben to take downstairs. Vanessa smiled as she thought of Shane and the outrageous suggestions he had made for their costumes. What would he come as, she found herself wondering. Something dashing, she was sure. A pirate, perhaps, or more likely a private eye like Matt. She gave her head an impatient little shake, annoyed with herself for thinking about him so often.

"Van?"

Something in Bettina's voice made Vanessa look up from the cheese she was cutting. "What is it?"

"Ben thinks one of the teachers in his school might have invited Todd tonight," she said with a note of apology in her voice. Ben and Todd were teachers in the same high school.

"You knew Ben was inviting a few of the teachers from his school? Well, Cindy asked him if it would be all right for her to bring a date. Ben realized later she probably meant Todd."

Vanessa lifted her shoulders in a shrug of resignation. "Don't worry about it," she said. "He probably won't show, and if he does—it won't be the first time I've bumped into him in public. It happens."

"But it bothers you," Bettina stated, knowing her friend.

"In a way, yes," Vanessa said honestly. "But it's more awkward than embarrassing—especially when someone whispers to his latest girlfriend that I'm his ex-wife. Anyway, I can handle it. He just doesn't mean that much to me any more." Any feelings of pain for Todd had long ago ceased. If anything, she felt only a mild regret that he had turned out to be so different from the man she'd thought him to be.

Bettina knew a great deal of what Vanessa had been through. "Are you sure, Van? I can always tell him to get lost. In fact, come to think of it, I'd love to tell him to get lost."

Vanessa smiled and shook her head. "I'm sure. Pass me that box of crackers, will you?"

The large family room in the basement was dimly lit and decorated for Halloween. Jack-o'-lanterns grinned ghoulishly from dark corners while rubber spiders bobbed from the ceiling on elastic strings, their dusty webs produced from a spray can. Dry ice, hidden behind the bar, emitted steamy wisps colored red by an overhead light.

Soon the guests began to arrive, their colorful costumes evoking admiration and laughter. Vanessa caught several puzzled looks and grinned, enjoying the feeling of not being recognized in a room full of friends. She stood in a dark corner nursing a drink, content for a while just to watch. It was amusing and absurd, this potpourri of disguises. People talked, laughed and danced together.

There was a sheikh and a hobo, witches and a bride; someone dressed as Santa Claus stood arm in arm with a hula dancer, while Charlie Chaplin, complete with thick black mustache and bowler hat, tried to get people to smell the brightly colored plastic flower on the lapel of his shabby suit.

Vanessa continued to hang back, studying each newcomer closely, hoping that Todd wouldn't show up, although disguised as she was, she might be able to avoid him if he did come. In spite of her assurances to Bettina, she hated running into him. He always managed to say something to embarrass her.

Charlie Chaplin appeared suddenly at her side, distracting her from her worries. "If you'll smell my flower, I'll let you bite my neck," he said, twitching his mustache.

Vanessa turned and bared her fangs in a grin. "If you promise not to squirt me, I promise not to draw blood."

"Vanessa?"

"Who?"

"It's you, Vanessa," Shane said confidently, lifting a strand of black nylon hair from her shoulders. "I can tell by your eyes—amber almonds, tinted with tiny flecks of green."

Vanessa took a sip of her drink and studied him with amusement. He was wearing a shabby, too-big suit jacket, long baggy pants and oversized well-worn shoes. A bowler hat set back on a wig, a wild disarray of dark curls, completed his costume. His lips twitched under a shaggy mustache.

"I like it," she said, meeting his eyes with a smile. "Though I kind of expected Matt Savage to show up."

"I left him between the pages of a book, where he belongs," Shane said. His eyes roved over her, lingering on the curves revealed by the well-fitted black dress. "You look—kinky," he said, "lurking in the shadows with the jack-o'-lantern flickering beside you. Do you bite?"

"Only when provoked."

He tilted his head to one side, exposing the strong column of his neck. "Please—tell me again, quick. What provokes you?"

"Shane Wilder, you're incorrigible." She pointed toward the center of the room. "If it's pain you're looking for, there's a cat over there who's dying to get her claws into you." Carla was dressed in a sleek, black body suit with pointed ears and a long bobbing tail. She had made no attempt to hide the fact that she was interested in Shane.

"I'm allergic to cats," Shane said.

"What about brides?" Vanessa asked slyly, pointing to Gail in her frothy white gown and veil.

"I break out in a rash," he said with a mock shudder. "I'll take my chances with a vampire any day."

"Well, this vampire volunteered for kitchen duty tonight," Vanessa said. "I have to go see if Bettina needs any help."

"Is there anything I can do?"

"Maybe Ben can use some help behind the bar," she said, realizing that Shane wouldn't know too many people that night. Serving drinks would help him to break the ice.

"Ben's the Viking looming in the red fog? Okay—I'll tell him you sent me. But Vanessa," he added, stopping her with a hand on her arm. "Don't become too duty-bound—I plan on dancing with you later."

"I won't, and I'll hold you to that dance," she said lightly, moving away with a smile. Wondering how someone dressed as ridiculously as Shane could still hold such appeal, she went upstairs to lend Bettina a hand.

When she returned with a tray of hot hors d'oeuvres, she saw that Shane was quite happily ensconced behind the bar with Ben. Judging from the laughter she could hear, the two of them were getting along quite well as they served drinks to a colorful throng of costumed characters. Carla had obviously recognized Shane and was busy entertaining him with her impression of a sinuous, purring cat.

She'll be snuggling up around his ankles in a moment, Vanessa thought as she passed around the tray. She smiled at a friendly, green-faced goblin and moved on. Gail would find him next and perch on a bar stool, demure in her white dress and breathless little girl's voice. It was the first time Vanessa had seen either of them at a staff party without a date in tow, and she was sure it was because they fancied their chances with Shane. Which one would be first?

"How's it going?" Bettina asked, coming up beside her.

"Pretty good. I put another pan of stuffed mushrooms in the oven. They should be ready by now."

"I'll see to them," Bettina said, taking the tray from her hands. "You're due for a break, Cinderella. Go rescue Prince Charming from that cat."

"Who—Ben?"

"No, Vanessa," Bettina said with exaggerated patience. "Shane."

"He doesn't look like he wants to be rescued."

"Rescue him anyway. Carla doesn't need another conquest and I wouldn't wish Gail on any man. Come on, girl! You didn't come to this party to pass around eats all night. Ask him to dance or something."

"Well—I'll go for a drink, anyway."

Bettina sighed. "It's a start, I suppose."

Vanessa leaned against the bar, smiling at Ben. He was as much her friend as Bettina was. "Hi, Ben," she said, feigning flirtatiousness. "How's life behind the bar?"

"Great," he said. "I think I missed my calling in life. This sure beats pounding history lessons into recalcitrant teenagers. Oh, and thanks for sending me Shane here. Not only has he promised to autograph my books, but he mixes a mean drink. We make a great team."

"Like Abbott and Costello," Shane said.

"Or the Marx Brothers minus a few," agreed Ben.

"How about Laurel and Hardy?" Shane asked, scrunching up his face as he lifted his hat to scratch the top of his head.

Vanessa laughed with a shake of her head. "Can I get a drink here, or is this strictly a comedy review?"

"One drink coming up," Ben said. "Something thick and red, don't you think, Shane? Something she can really sink her teeth into."

"A Bloody Mary," Shane suggested.

"Let's make it a Caesar," Ben said. "It's got more of a bite."

Vanessa groaned. "Just a glass of wine, please."

"Red, of course," Shane said, pouring.

"Of course," Vanessa said, taking the glass from him with a smile of thanks.

Carla spoke up suddenly, sounding a bit petulant. "Isn't Todd coming tonight?" she asked with a sly glance at Vanessa. "I'm sure he's dying to see you, Vanessa." Ignoring Ben's frown, she turned to smile widely at Shane. "Come on," she demanded with a little pout. "You promised to dance with me."

"So I did," Shane said. He took the hand Carla held out to him, but his eyes, narrow with curiosity, watched Vanessa's still face. As Carla tugged impatiently on his hand, he let himself be led to the center of the room where several couples were dancing.

Vanessa watched as Carla moved close to Shane with a sinuous wiggle of her lithe body. She turned away, catching the look of concern in Ben's eyes.

"I doubt that Todd'll show up, Van," he assured her, his voice low as he leaned toward her. "He knows he's not exactly welcome." He picked up his glass and took a swallow of Scotch. "What's gotten into Carla tonight anyway?" he asked. "She's not usually so—catty."

"She wants to sink those claws of hers into Shane," Vanessa said a touch dryly as she sat on the bar stool Carla had vacated.

"Poor guy," Ben said with a shake of his shaggy blond head.

"Does he look worried?" Vanessa murmured with a quick glance toward the dancing couple.

"Maybe not, but he doesn't know Carla like I do. She's a bit *too* hungry, if you know—" He broke off as a portly gray-whiskered tramp came up to the bar. "Hi, Jack—what can I get you?"

Vanessa listened absently to their conversation, running a finger around the rim of her glass. It was beginning to look as though Todd wouldn't show up after all. She doubted that it was out of concern for her feelings—he had never shown any such consideration before. Regardless, it was a relief to know that she wouldn't have to face him. He had never really understood why she hadn't been able to forgive him, and he still harbored resentment over the fact that she had divorced him. On the few occasions they had been thrown together at some social function, he had never failed to make one or two smug comments about his latest conquests, adding in a suggestive voice that maybe they could get together later for a drink—or something.

Vanessa grimaced a little at the memory of their last encounter. Had he changed so much from the man she'd thought she loved, or had she been totally blind? She raised her glass to her lips and took a sip of wine.

Suddenly Shane stood beside her. Reaching across the bar, he picked up the drink he had left there and took a swallow. Leaning an elbow on the padded edge of the bar top, he smiled crookedly beneath the absurd bushy mustache.

"Where's the cat?" Vanessa asked, looking up at him, a smile playing on her lips.

Shane gave a shrug of disinterest. "Off to the sandbox, I think." He touched a finger to the scarlet drop glistening at the corner of her mouth. "Who's Todd?" he demanded suddenly. "An old boyfriend?"

Vanessa moved her face away from the sting of his touch. "Ex-husband," she murmured.

His eyebrows shot up in surprise. "You were married?"

She looked away from the curiosity lighting his eyes. "Briefly."

"How long is briefly?"

"Just under two years."

"You must have been very young."

"I was nineteen when we got married—a very young nineteen."

Shane studied the curve of her averted face. "If you want to tell me it's none of my business, feel free, but—what happened?"

"I found out our views on fidelity clashed badly." That was all she had meant to say, but found herself adding, "He told me he was going to a party one night. I hadn't planned on going, but I changed my mind and decided to surprise him." She looked down, swirling the wine in her glass before taking a drink. "He'd neglected to tell me it was a private party for two."

"And you walked in on them." Shane's voice was gentle.

Vanessa's eyes closed briefly and she nodded. "Maybe if I'd just heard about it, I could have ignored it, or forgiven him. But to actually see him—" She broke off and turned away from his sympathetic eyes, already wishing she hadn't said so much.

"It must have been rough," he said, his hand touching her arm lightly. He had heard the echo of shame and humiliation behind her matter-of-fact tone. "But if you want my opinion, the guy must be a jerk."

Vanessa looked at him and grinned unexpectedly. "Actually, he is," she agreed. "But in all fairness, he was a lot of fun when we first met. We had some good times together. My mistake lay in marrying him."

"Marriage is a mistake a lot of people make," Shane said, a frown cutting sharply across his brow.

"You say that as though you've had the experience. Were you married?"

"No," he said shortly. "That's something I plan to avoid. I learned all I need to know about marriage from observing my parents." He straightened up as he saw Carla coming down the stairs. "I feel a sudden return of my allergies," he murmured. "Dance with me?"

"All right." Vanessa slid off the stool, smoothing the close-fitting material of her dress over her hips. Catching a glimpse of Carla's glare, she smiled and turned as Shane took her in his arms, the soft, supple rhythm of the reggae beat guiding their movements.

He held her close, the hardness of his chest against her. She felt surprisingly relaxed. She looked up to smile at him, but instead, burst into laughter.

"What's so funny?" he demanded.

"Us." She giggled. "Everyone." She made a sweeping gesture with her hand. "I've never seen such an odd assortment of couples."

"An assortment of odd couples." He chuckled in agreement. "I don't know about them, but I've had just about enough of being in disguise. This mustache is making me crazy."

Vanessa took a corner of the mustache and gently peeled it off. "Better?" she asked with a teasing smile.

He rubbed under his nose and took a deep breath. "Much better."

"If you can go without the mustache, I can go without the fangs," she said, and pulled them out. "I was starting to lisp after that last drink anyway. Now, if only I could get rid of the wig. It's beginning to itch."

Shane took off his hat and gave his head a little shake, setting his own wig quivering. "I'll take off mine if you'll take off yours," he said, his eyebrows quirking suggestively.

"You go first."

"All right." He took her arm and steered her toward a corner of the room then pulled off his wig with a flourish and stuffed it into a pocket. He ran his fingers through his own dark curls and grinned. "That feels a lot better. Your turn."

Vanessa pulled off her wig, setting it on a side table as she fumbled with the pins holding up her hair.

"Here," Shane said. "Let me." His fingers searched for pins, releasing her curls to tumble around her shoulders. Gently he fluffed her hair, pushing it back at the temples.

Vanessa stood still, almost mesmerized by his soft, sensitive touch.

"Much, much better," he murmured, pushing aside a curl that lay just above her breast. "The makeup might leave a lot to be desired, but you're much prettier as a blonde."

"Sort of blonde," she corrected, left a little breathless by his touch. "That's what my mother used to call it." She smiled longingly at the memory.

Shane studied the expressions flitting across her face. "Your parents aren't living?"

Vanessa shook her head. "They died in a car accident, along with Marcie's parents—my brother and his wife."

"I'm sorry," Shane said gently. "That must have been a very hard time for you."

Vanessa's eyes darkened briefly. "It was, but it was a long time ago. We've learned to live with it."

Shane pulled her into his arms and began to dance slowly. Vanessa relaxed against the solid wall of his chest, feeling his warm breath against her hair as his hands stroked her lower back, coming to rest on the curve of her hips. His hold tightened as he pulled her closer still. His hard thighs pushed up against the silky fabric of her dress gave her a sharp stab of excitement in the pit of her stomach. Alarmed by her growing arousal, she pushed away from him and stepped back.

"I—I have to go see if Bettina needs any help," she said, turning away from his intense stare. Did he look at all women like that, as though he found them endlessly fascinating? She glanced back with a quick, somewhat apologetic smile and hurried toward the stairs.

Damn it, she thought with a frown. She hadn't wanted to feel that stirring at his touch, to acknowledge her aching desire to have his arms close around her as his lips found and clung to hers.

It would be so easy to fall for him, she thought, going through the kitchen to the upstairs bathroom. The attraction was definitely there. He was a very likable, extremely sexy man. Yes, she could fall hard.

She splashed warm soapy water on her face until the heavy makeup was gone, then she toweled dry. She knew the attraction was mutual. Shane made no attempt to hide the fact that he found her desirable. She had to control her feelings before they carried her away.

She sighed and tugged a comb through her hair, looking in the mirror with worried eyes. She would have to be cautious. Shane was attractive to many women, there could be no doubt about that. Gail and Carla were downstairs at that moment, vying for his too-willing attention, and there would be others, she knew. Men like Shane Wilder were never without women. If she wasn't careful, she would end up being just one of many, and there was no way she was going to let that happen to her again. She had learned her lesson well.

She slipped quietly back downstairs and joined a small group, trying to involve herself in their chatter, but her real attention was focused on Shane.

She watched him unobtrusively, noting his popularity with both the men and the women. Especially the women, she thought with a wry twist to her lips. Watching him laughing and dancing almost continuously was almost like reliving the parties she had been to with Todd. How often had she spent entire evenings talking quietly in a corner while Todd danced and entertained some other woman, trying to convince herself it didn't hurt? She frowned sharply and turned away as Gail snuggled into Shane's arms for a slow dance. It's not the same thing, she told herself firmly. Todd was my husband. Shane is nothing to me.

"IT WAS A GREAT PARTY, Bettina," Shane said as people began to leave. "Thanks for having me."

"We're glad you could be here," Bettina said. "No, no," she added adamantly as Shane began to help Vanessa pick up sticky glasses and overflowing ashtrays. "You two have done enough tonight. Leave everything as is. Ben and I will clean up tomorrow."

"I'll give you a hand when I bring Haili back," Vanessa offered.

"Don't make it too early," Ben put in. "I plan on sleeping late."

"Mm—that sounds like a good idea." Vanessa smothered a yawn. "I'd better be going before I fall asleep."

"Are you driving?" Shane asked.

She shook her head. "I never drive when I've been drinking. I'm taking a cab."

"I'll drive you," Shane stated firmly. "No—it's no problem," he added, cutting through her protests. "It's not far out of my way, and I haven't had anything stronger than ginger ale tonight—Ben can vouch for that."

"That's right, Van," Ben agreed. "Even my most exotic concoctions didn't tempt him. He's safe."

Vanessa looked at Shane warily. Oh, no, he's not, she thought with a silent conviction. But she accepted his offer, conscious of the pleased smile Bettina exchanged with Ben.

It was a short drive, made in a comfortable silence. Shane stopped the car in front of her house.

"I'll see you to the door," he said. "Do you have your keys?"

"Right here." She dangled the key chain from her fingers. "But you don't have to get out. I'll be okay."

"I'll see you to the door," he repeated, opening his door and getting out.

The night was still, crisp and cool. Frost had settled on the grass and sidewalks, glistening under the glow from the streetlights. Vanessa pursed her lips and blew a snowy plume into the air.

"Winter's coming," she said, pushing open the gate to the yard.

"Soon it'll be time for skating and skiing and long, cozy nights by the fire."

"You almost make it sound good."

"It is," he said assuredly and added smugly, "but then, I work at home and don't have to go out to start a frozen car at the crack of dawn on those frigid January mornings."

"Winter would be pleasurable—almost—without that," Vanessa acknowledged, turning her key in the lock and pushing open the door a crack. "Thank you for driving me home, Shane."

"You're welcome. Vanessa..."

"Yes?" she murmured.

"I enjoy your company," he said, his voice low. "I want to see you again. Other than in the library," he added quickly, anticipating her response.

Vanessa studied his face under the porch light. "I don't think so," she said finally. She knew she had to try and protect herself from this man.

Shane gave an exaggerated sigh. "It's a good thing I enjoy a challenge," he said, unperplexed by her refusal.

"Does that mean if I'd said yes, you wouldn't want to go out with me any more?" she asked with a teasing smile.

"Try me and see," he dared.

"Shane—let's just be friends," she said impulsively.

"Friends?" He ran a finger along the fine curve of her jaw.

"Friends," she repeated, feeling breathless under his steady touch.

His fingers hooked under her chin and he tilted her face. "And how do you say good-night to your friends?" he asked softly, his mouth moving closer to hers.

Vanessa swayed toward him, feeling the warmth of his breath against her lips. Then, with a little frown and a shake of her head, she stepped back and held out her hand. "Like this," she said. "Good night, Shane."

Chuckling, he took her fingers in his hand. "Good night, Vanessa," he said. Raising her hand to his lips, he pressed a kiss on the soft skin of her inner wrist, lingering on the pulse that quickened to his touch. "I'll see you soon."

Vanessa watched him go down the steps before entering the house, shaking her head ruefully. It had been a long, long time since she had felt the sweet stirrings of arousal. If he was persistent, and he gave every sign of being so, could she resist him for long?

Shane might love lightly and without commitment, but she couldn't, not without losing the balance she had struggled so hard to regain after Todd. She rubbed her wrist where the skin still tingled from the touch of Shane's lips and sighed, hoping she could find the strength to fight the attraction she felt for him.

Shane Wilder was a very tempting man, but falling for him was going to leave her wide open for heartache.

CHAPTER FOUR

"SOMETHING'S BOTHERING TOMMY." Shane pulled up a chair beside Vanessa's desk. "Do you have any idea what it might be?"

Vanessa looked up from the report she was writing and shook her head. "I hardly saw him today," she said. She had been helping a grade-six class research eighteenth-century Canadian explorers during most of Shane's session with Tommy. Seeing the sharp line of concern cutting his brow, she asked, "What makes you think something is wrong?"

Shane ran a hand through his hair and shrugged. "He was different today—unattentive, sullen, even. His clothes were dirty and he obviously hadn't had a bath in a while. Something is wrong in that kid's life, Vanessa," he added with quiet conviction.

"Did you ask him about it?"

"I tried. All he'd do was just turn away or shrug. He wasn't talking. Even his eyes were expressionless."

"Maybe he's just having an off day," Vanessa suggested.

Shane shook his head. "I don't think so. There's more to it than that—I can feel it. Do you think Bettina will let me have his home phone number? I'd like to talk to his mother."

Vanessa could see the concern darkening his eyes. "You really are worried, aren't you?"

He nodded, drumming the tips of his fingers on the desktop. "I've worked with him twice a week for over a month now," he said. "And each time he's been more responsive, friendlier. But today—" He lifted his shoulders. "—today was different. I know something is wrong and I'd like to try and help him."

Vanessa nodded slowly, appreciating his willingness to become involved. It was a too rare quality these days. "I've got some spare time," she said, pushing back her chair. "Why don't we go see what Gail has to say?"

According to Gail, Tommy had been absent the day before and late that morning. "And his clothes look like they've been slept in," she added, her nose wrinkling with a look of distaste. "Usually he's fairly neat and clean. Did you try to talk to him?" she asked Shane.

"Yes," Shane assured her. "He isn't saying anything."

"Oh, well," Gail said dismissingly. "It probably isn't much. Maybe his mother had a party—one of those kinds that lasts three days." You know these people, her expression said.

"Tommy's mother isn't like that," Vanessa said with a frown.

Gail shrugged. "Well—if he says anything, I'll let you know. In the meantime—" She inclined her head toward her classroom, grimacing at the growing hubbub coming from behind the closed door. "See you later, Shane." She smiled sweetly.

For once Shane seemed oblivious to the openly flirtatious message in Gail's wide blue eyes. "Yeah, sure," he muttered, turning away.

"She didn't seem too bothered," he said to Vanessa as they walked down the hall.

Vanessa tried to be fair, though she'd often thought that Gail didn't pay enough attention to kids like Tommy. "She's got close to thirty students in that room," she said. "Many with problems a lot more severe than Tommy's."

"I suppose. But—" Shane shrugged and let the subject drop.

She was convinced Gail would do much better away from the chaos of an inner-city school. A suburban school and the subtle problems of middle-class students would be more in her line.

"Look," she said as they approached the library, "I've got to get back to work. Why don't you talk to Bettina and see what she has to say?"

"I'll do that." Shane nodded. "Vanessa—" He hesitated. "I know it might seem like I'm overreacting...I don't know, maybe I am. But—"

"It's okay, Shane." Vanessa smiled and laid a hand briefly on his arm. "I'm glad you care enough to bother. Let me know what Bettina says, okay?"

"Will do." With a somewhat absent smile, he left her at the door to the library and went to the office.

Vanessa sat behind her desk, tapping her pen thoughtfully on the unfinished report in front of her. She was a little surprised by Shane's reaction. Most people would have let things ride, waited a day or two to see if the problems would work out on their own. But she didn't fault Shane for his quick concern. In fact, she thought it added an admirable dimension to his character.

"Well?" she asked a short time later as Shane returned to her desk.

"They have no phone," he said, sitting down. "But Bettina gave me the address and suggested I go over and talk to his mother. She also suggested that it might be better if someone from the school came with me. She thought maybe Gail, but I think your presence would be more beneficial. Will you come with me, Vanessa?"

"Of course I will," she answered without hesitation. "When would you like to go?"

"This evening," he said. "About six-thirty? I'll pick you up."

Vanessa nodded her agreement and then asked impulsively, "Would you like to come over for supper first?"

"I'd like that," he replied promptly. "What time?"

"Make it about five," she said and then added, "I can't guarantee what we'll be having. It depends on what Gran takes out of the freezer."

"Anything will do," he said, standing up. "I've got to go, Vanessa." He smiled, his eyes light as they rested briefly on hers. "See you later."

"See you later," she echoed, watching him leave. So much, she thought, for my big plans of keeping him distant. If anything, she acknowledged with reluctance, she was glad for the excuse. She'd been avoiding him since the Halloween party.

It was just after four when Vanessa parked her car in the garage and let herself in through the kitchen door.

"Hi, Gran. I'm—" She stopped short and stared in surprise as Shane turned from the counter and grinned at her.

"Hello, dear," he drawled, his eyes gleaming. "Did you have a hard day at the office?"

"Oh, it was fairly normal," Vanessa answered, her lips twitching with laughter. "Marcos threw up on the magazine rack, wiping out three months of issues of *National Geographic*. After that was cleaned up, I found someone had written a rather nasty word all over my chalkboard— misspelled yet." She dropped her books on the kitchen table and shrugged off her coat, wondering why he had arrived so early, not that she minded. "Where's Gran?"

"On the phone. What did you do?" he asked, leaning back against the countertop, his arms crossed over his chest. "About the swear word."

"Added the missing letter and told them that if they really must write such words, they should at least spell them right."

"That's a different approach." Shane chuckled. He turned back to the counter and finished slicing a carrot. "Hungry?" he asked.

Vanessa nodded, her fingers dodging the knife for a piece of carrot. "Shane, what are you doing in my kitchen slicing up vegetables?"

"Isn't it obvious? I'm cooking supper," he said, pushing the carrots into a neat little pile with the blade of the knife.

"Why?"

"I volunteered."

"Volunteered—or got shanghaied by my grandmother?"

He chuckled. "A little of both. I thought all grandmothers loved to cook? Anyway, I'd phoned to ask if there was anything I could bring and she suggested that I come over early. One thing led to another and—" He looked at her closely. "You don't mind, do you?" he asked suddenly.

"Not if you're a good cook," she joked, surprised at how much she didn't mind. "What are you making?"

"Stir-fried vegetables and chicken in almond sauce," he answered. "Quick and tasty."

"So much tastier than what I had in mind," Cora said, coming in through the swinging doors. "Wasn't it nice of Shane to offer to make supper?" she asked Vanessa.

"How much of that offer was the result of some rather broad hints?" Vanessa asked dryly.

"Not much, dear." Cora's hazel eyes twinkled. "Shane catches on very quickly. All I had to do was mention that when you called, you said not to bother starting anything, but to wait until you got home."

"I think I like this better," Vanessa said, snatching a piece of broccoli from a neatly organized pile and snapping it between her teeth. "Do you need any help?" she asked, looking at Shane out of the corner of her eye.

"If he does, I'll help him." Cora said. "Why don't you go and change your clothes?"

"Okay, Gran." Vanessa caught Shane's wink over top of her grandmother's silver hair and smiled. "Just be careful she doesn't ruin anything, Shane. I'm starving!"

Marcie came in the front door as Vanessa started up the stairs to her bedroom.

"Hi, Aunt Van," she said, dropping her gym bag full of schoolbooks on the floor beside the door. She pushed a strand of windblown hair back from her face, her eyes sparkling above cold-reddened cheeks.

"Hi, kiddo." Vanessa smiled affectionately. "How was your day?"

"Pretty good. We had a volleyball practice after school— there's a game Thursday night." She hung her coat in the hall closet, noticing Shane's jacket. "Who's here?"

"Shane. He's staying for supper—which, by the way, Gran has him cooking. Could you please set the table while I change?"

"Sure. In the dining room?"

"No—the kitchen table will do. We're having a quick supper, then Shane and I are going to visit the mother of the boy Shane is working with. Shane's a bit worried about him," she added.

"Oh. So then this isn't a date or anything?" There was a note of disappointment in Marcie's voice.

Not another one, Vanessa thought wryly. "No, Marcie," she said. "Bettina suggested that someone from the school go with him. I'm that someone. That's all."

"But you do like him," Marcie persisted.

"I suppose I do. As a—a friend. Why?"

Marcie shrugged. "Just wondering." Her tone was casual. She headed to the kitchen. "I'll go set the table."

Vanessa hurried up the stairs and took a short, refreshing shower. She pulled her damp hair back and tied it loosely with a scarf, brushing the ends into soft, gold-tipped curls. She slipped into snug-fitting black jeans, which emphasized her long-legged figure, and an oversized cherry-red sweater, pushing up the sleeves. She took one final look in the mirror, and dabbed on a touch of lip gloss and just a hint of blush.

She shook her head as she turned away, laughing a bit at herself. For all her awareness of the upheaval involvement with Shane would bring to her well-ordered life, she was glad he was there. She would just have to be careful to keep the visit impersonal and friendly.

She ran downstairs and pushed open the kitchen door, taking a deep breath. "It smells great in here," she said. There was an aroma of garlic, spices and rice wine. "You may just be a good cook after all." She smiled at Shane. "Can I taste?" she asked, peering into the sizzling wok.

Shane dipped a spoon into the bubbling sauce, catching a slivered almond on the tip. Lifting it to his mouth, he blew gently to cool it and then offered the spoon to her.

Feeling self-conscious under his lazy, heavy-lidded gaze, Vanessa delicately took the spoon and put it into her mouth. "Mm—that's delicious. I'm impressed. Tell me—do you do windows?"

His eyes gleamed wickedly. "No. But I—" He stopped, looking across the room to Cora and Marcie, who were watching the exchange with unabashed interest. "—do floors," he finished, his eyes laughing, letting her know that wasn't even close to what he had been going to say.

As they sat down to eat, a ray from the setting sun found its way through a corner window, giving the kitchen a warm, golden glow. It stretched across the round maple table, highlighting the blue-and-white floral-patterned china and copper-bottomed pots, which hung on the brick wall opposite the table. The atmosphere, redolent with the aroma of good food, was cozy, happy.

Shane was good company. He teased gently, joked often and fit in easily. Cora and Marcie obviously liked him a lot.

When the meal was finished, they sat sipping cups of fragrant lotus-blossom tea.

"Marcie and I will clear up," Cora said, after a glance at the clock on the wall. "You two had better be going."

Shane put down his cup. "That was a great meal," he said. "Thank you for having me."

"You're the one who should be thanked," Cora said. "You did all the cooking."

"There's more to a good meal than the food." Shane smiled charmingly at Cora. "Good company is just as important."

Cora returned his smile, obviously pleased. "You can bring this one back any time, Vanessa," she said. "Such a nice, polite young man!"

Shane looked at Vanessa, his expression smug. See? he seemed to be saying. Vanessa made the tiniest of faces at him before pushing her chair away from the table.

"We really should be going," she said. "I shouldn't be back too late, Gran."

"Take your time," Cora urged. "I hope everything's okay."

"Thank you," Shane said, standing up. "And I'll be seeing you two again soon."

"I'm looking forward to it." Cora winked at Vanessa. "Make sure he keeps his word."

Vanessa merely smiled at her grandmother as she stooped to kiss her cheek. "See you later," she said, and left the kitchen, followed by Shane.

"My grandmother is matchmaking," she muttered as she reached into the hall closet for their coats.

"I can go along with that," Shane said with his lazy grin as he took his jacket from her.

Vanessa slipped her arms into her sweater jacket and zipped it up. "To Gran, matchmaking means marriage," she explained, glancing at him sideways.

"Oh." There was an expression of consternation on his face. "Maybe we could just be friends after all."

Vanessa had to laugh. "What have you got against marriage?" she asked, looking in the hall mirror to pull on a beret that matched her emerald-green sweater.

"Everything," he answered promptly.

Vanessa turned away from the mirror. "Seriously, Shane." She was sure that he was going to make a flippant reply, but suddenly his eyes darkened and his face looked harder than she had ever seen it before.

"It traps people," he said finally, his voice flat. "It destroys love."

Vanessa felt a little pang of disappointment. He really seemed to believe what he was saying. "Your parents weren't happy together," she stated gently.

He shook his head curtly. "Are you ready?" he asked abruptly. "We'd better get going."

She nodded, accepting that it wasn't something he wanted to talk about. Picking up her purse, she followed him out to his car.

THE SMALL, RUN-DOWN DUPLEX in the core of Winnipeg was an unhappy sight. The brick siding was ripped in spots and a rickety, unstable-looking veranda leaned drunkenly away from the front wall. An ancient elm tree had taken over what front yard there was, its twisted limbs reaching over the roof.

Vanessa climbed the front steps, followed by Shane, and opened the tattered screen door, as Shane knocked loudly on the inner door.

A puffy-eyed young woman eventually came to the door. "What d'ya want?"

"We'd like to speak to Mrs. Hawkes," Shane said pleasantly. "Tommy's mother. Is she in?"

Her unkempt head shook negatively. "Uh-uh. What'd he do anyway? Are you cops or somethin'?"

"We're from Tommy's school," Vanessa spoke up. "And he hasn't done anything—we'd just like a word with his mother. Do you know when she'll be back?"

The woman shrugged. "Next week, maybe. I don't know for sure."

"Are you looking after Tommy?" Shane asked, frowning.

"Yeah, sort of. His aunt was, but she got sick and had to go to the hospital, so I'm staying. I got kicked out of my last place and needed a place anyway."

Vanessa gave Shane a quick, worried look. "Could we speak to Tommy, please?"

"He's out somewhere."

"Out? Where?" Shane asked.

"I don't know—downtown maybe." She obviously really didn't care. "What's with all the questions, anyway?"

Sensing her growing antagonism, Shane smiled placatingly. "We're just a bit concerned with Tommy's behavior in school this week."

"Yeah? He's pretty bratty, eh?" Her face was more awake-looking now, and she stared at Shane, her growing interest undisguised. "I hadda spank him yesterday. He got real rude when my boyfriend came over. Earl just got outta jail and we hadn't had a—a party in a long time." She smiled slyly and winked knowingly at Shane. "I hadda show him a good time, y'know."

Vanessa saw Shane's face tighten almost imperceptibly and knew that he, too, was struggling to keep his anger and contempt from showing.

"Is there any way we can contact Tommy's mother?" he asked, his voice smooth with restraint.

"Uh-uh. She went back to Sterling for a funeral for one of her old friends. I don't have a phone number or nothin'."

"I see. My name is Shane, by the way," he said with a sudden, charming smile. "What's yours?"

She pushed back her shoulders, her full breasts straining against her T-shirt. "Nadine," she answered, her brown eyes narrowed and glistening.

"Nadine," Shane repeated. "That's a very pretty name."

I've heard that line before, Vanessa thought, stepping back unobtrusively, watching Nadine preen under Shane's smile. He would get the answers they wanted.

"Nadine," he said, "what's the name of Tommy's aunt—the one in the hospital?"

"Alma—Alma Spence."

"I suppose she's at the Health Sciences?" Shane questioned.

"Yeah. You gonna go talk to her?"

"I might, Nadine."

"Well, if you do, you tell her I'm not gonna stick around here baby-sitting that snotty-nosed brat much longer. Earl and me got things to do."

"Is Earl staying here, too?" Shane asked.

"He was for a couple of days. Making up for lost time, y'know." She smiled archly. "Say—d'ya want to come in for a drink? I got some beer." She smiled at Shane and then looked doubtfully at Vanessa.

"No, thank you, Nadine." Shane was still charmingly polite. "We have to be going." As he turned away with Vanessa, he looked over his shoulder. "Do you have any idea at all where Tommy might be?"

"Naw. Hanging around downtown somewhere, probably. See you around, eh?" She shut the door.

"Unreal," Vanessa said with a shake of her head.

"Too real," Shane said grimly. "No wonder Tommy has been acting the way he has."

"What are we going to do now?"

"I'm going to take you home," Shane said, "and then I'm going to go look for Tommy. The poor little guy must really need a friend just now."

Vanessa stopped beside the car and looked at Shane seriously. "Maybe we should report this to the authorities."

"It's too soon for that." He frowned and shook his head adamantly. "Neither Tommy nor his mother deserves that. She didn't leave Nadine in charge. The aunt did, in what appears to have been an emergency." He opened the car door. "Get in, Vanessa. I'm taking you home."

"I'm coming with you," she insisted.

"Vanessa, please."

"No, Shane, I want to. I'm worried about Tommy, too, you know. Especially after what we just witnessed." She gestured toward the house. "Besides, the way things are these days, your motives could be misunderstood. It would be better if I was with you."

He studied her closely for a moment, his face still under the glare of the streetlight. "What about you—do you understand my motives?"

"I think so. You're worried about a little boy who's missing his mother and out wandering the streets alone because he dreads coming home to that—that half-sloshed bimbo. And I think," she added softly, with sudden insight, "that you know exactly what he's feeling."

A muscle twitched in the side of his face. "I do." He turned away from her, hiding distant shades of pain. "But it was my father I was missing and the woman wasn't a bimbo." He laughed shortly. "She was my mother. But half-sloshed nonetheless."

Vanessa took his hand and squeezed it in silent sympathy. "Let's go find Tommy," she said.

They left the car parked in front of the duplex and began walking up the street.

"We lived not far from here," Shane said suddenly. He was staring straight ahead as he began to talk. "In one of those old brick apartment buildings. It was all we could afford after my father left." He was silent for a moment and then went on. "I thought it would be better when he was gone—no more fighting...but it wasn't. The constant tension was gone, but my mother was so bitter. My father ran off with another woman, and my mother never forgave him for that. She started to drink. Not every day, but often enough. I never knew how I'd find her when I got home from school."

"So you started staying away," Vanessa said, her voice soft with sympathy for the vulnerable little boy he had been. "Where did you go?"

"To the library a lot, especially at first. Thank God for books," he added with a bitter little laugh. "When I got into my later teens, I started hanging around the arcades, growing more streetwise and a hell of a lot more cynical. I came damned close to ruining my life."

"But you didn't. What happened?"

"There was one person who cared, really cared about what happened to me," he said. "My Uncle Henry—my mother's uncle, actually. He was a retired schoolteacher. He straightened me out and turned me around at a time when no one else could be bothered."

"Is he still living?"

Shane shook his head. "No. He died just over a year ago, after a lengthy illness. That's the main reason I stayed on in Winnipeg—so he wouldn't be alone at the end. I was the only real family he had." He kicked at a stone, watching it shoot ahead, rustling through the scattered leaves along the sidewalk. "I was never able to repay him for all he did for me, but—"

"You can repay it in kind," Vanessa finished for him, sliding her hand through his arm. "Tommy is lucky to have you as a friend."

Shane looked at her and smiled, patting the hand that rested on his arm. "Let's just hope that we can find him tonight," he said. "I want him to know he's not alone with that—that . . ."

"Half-sloshed bimbo and her con boyfriend. Where do you suggest we start looking?"

"He'll be someplace warm, someplace where he can blend into the crowd—probably at the mall in Eaton Place. We'll start there and work our way down Portage to the Bay."

Christmas lights were strung along Portage Avenue, their brilliant colors glittering against the dark, frosty night. Stores were gaily decorated and people scurried in and out, hurrying through their shopping. To Vanessa, it seemed an impossible task to find one small boy in the midst of all that activity.

They started their search in the mall at Eaton Place.

"There are so many kids," Vanessa murmured, watching a group of young teenagers in the restaurant area. "They should be at home."

"Their homes are often intolerable," Shane answered grimly, looking round through narrowed, searching eyes.

"They'd rather be here with their friends where they feel comfortable and accepted. The hangouts may have changed since I was their age, but the reasons for being there haven't." He took another look around the bright area with its plastic stools and tables. "Tommy isn't here," he said. "Let's check out the lower level."

They spotted Tommy from the escalator. He was hanging over the side of a case on display just outside a pet store, grinning at the puppy licking his hand. Instinctively Vanessa stayed back, letting Shane approach first.

"Hello, Tommy," he said, kneeling down beside the boy, his elbows on the edge of the case. "That's a nice little puppy, isn't it?"

"Yeah." Tommy gave him a sideways glance. "He keeps on licking me all the time."

"He must like you," Shane said reassuringly. "I went to your house tonight, Tommy," he stated casually.

Tommy looked down nervously, saying nothing.

"I'm really sorry that your mom isn't home," Shane continued. "And that your aunt is in the hospital. I'm sure it's hard for you. I don't think Nadine looks after you very well."

Tommy risked a quick look.

Shane smiled gently. "But I don't think that you should be here all by yourself. Miss Evans and I came to take you home."

Startled, Tommy looked over his shoulder at Vanessa. She smiled warmly at him. "Hello, Tommy."

He looked quickly back at the pup. "'lo," he mumbled shyly.

"I'll bet you're feeling tired and hungry," she said. "Will you let us take you home?"

Tommy scowled. "No. I won't go."

Shane gave Vanessa a quick concerned look then turned toward Tommy. "Why? It will be okay."

"I don't like that man." Tears began welling up in the child's eyes.

"Do you mean Earl?" Shane questioned.

Tommy nodded, sniffling. "Can you tell me why you don't like him, Tommy?"

Tommy lifted his thin shoulders in a shrug. "They get drunk an' stuff."

"Well, he wasn't there when Miss Evans and I stopped by just a little while ago," Shane told him. "Maybe he won't come back tonight. Let's go see." Shane stood up and held out his hand and after a moment of hesitation, Tommy put his hand into it.

"Atta boy, Tommy," Shane said with a warm smile, squeezing the small hand gently. "I promise everything will be okay. Coming, Ms Evans?" His smile was warm for her, too.

"Coming, Mr. Wilder," she answered, returning his smile openly as she took Tommy's other hand in hers.

By the time they had walked back to Tommy's house, it was late. Light was streaming through a crack in the curtain over the living-room window and they could hear the sound of raucous laughter from within. Shane's lips were tight as he knocked loudly on the door.

Nadine opened the door after a few minutes, blinking drunkenly at them. "Jus' in time for the party," she slurred. "Earl's friend got some rye. We're gonna have a good time!" She threw the door open wide, hanging onto it as she swayed off balance.

"I brought Tommy home," Shane said coldly.

"Huh? Oh, geez—get in an' get to bed, Tommy," she scolded.

Shane's arm went reassuringly around Tommy's shoulder, indicating to the boy not to move.

"Hey, Nadine!" A man's voice bellowed from the living room. "Shut the goddamn door, will ya!" A thin man lurched into the hallway, his greasy blond hair falling lankly around his sallow face. "It's colder than a witch's—" He stopped abruptly, his eyes narrowing at the sight of Shane and Vanessa standing in the doorway with Tommy huddled between them. "Cops?" he asked Nadine.

"Nah—teachers or somethin'. They brought the kid back."

"But he won't be staying," Shane said, his hand tightening on Tommy's shoulder. "He's coming with me."

"You social workers or what?" the man asked.

"We're Tommy's friends," Vanessa said, her expression plainly showing her distaste for what she was seeing.

"Friends?" the man mimicked, switching his gimlet gaze to her. "Don't give you no rights."

Vanessa returned his stare coldly. "Perhaps we'll let the police decide who has what rights." She looked at Shane. "Do you think your friend Jack—Sergeant Preston—is on duty tonight?"

"As a matter of fact, I believe he is," Shane said, his voice relaxing to a drawl. "I'll bet he'd be interested in checking out this little party. What do you say, Earl? Should I give him a call?"

Earl glanced nervously over his shoulder toward the living room. "Uh—Nadine, let's let the kid go." His tongue darted over his lips. "Who needs the hassle anyway?"

"I'm gonna tell your mom, Tommy." Nadine scowled, wagging a finger at the boy. "Causing all this trouble an' stuff."

"No—I'm going to tell his mother," Shane said, his voice harsh. "If there has been any trouble, you've caused it, not Tommy, and I'll make sure she knows it." Without another word, he turned away, ushering Tommy and Vanessa to the car.

"Now what?" Vanessa asked as they settled into the car, Tommy on the seat between them.

"First things first. Did you eat tonight, Tommy?"

Tommy shook his head.

"Would you like to come with us and have something to eat?"

"Okay." Tommy was silent for a moment, staring at his hands. "I don't like people getting drunk."

"Neither do I, Tommy," Shane said.

Tommy looked up at him. "Do you get drunk?"

"No." Shane smiled, gently reassuring.

Tommy stared at him for a moment, the light from the street lamp making his thin little face appear pale. He dropped his head abruptly with a stifled sob.

Her heart contracting with pity, Vanessa put an arm around his shoulders and pulled him to her. He stiffened, then relaxed against her with a shudder.

"Oh, Shane," she murmured, her eyes dark with concern. "He's shaking like a leaf." Her arms tightened around him and she rubbed his back comfortingly. "He's chilled right through, poor little soul. I don't think he can take much more tonight."

Shane started the engine and flicked on the heater as he pulled away from the curb. "My place is only a couple of minutes from here," he said. "He needs a hot bath and some food right away."

Vanessa was about to suggest they take Tommy to her place, but his shuddering body and the silent tears she could see streaking his face told her he'd had enough. The sooner he was fed and put into a warm bed, the better it would be. And, she realized, he didn't need the added stress of meeting Cora and Marcie, no matter how sympathetic they would be.

"By the way," Shane said suddenly to Vanessa. "I liked that part about my friend Sergeant Preston. I was just beginning to wonder what Matt Savage would have done in a situation like that." He smiled a little grimly. "You saved us a lot of trouble."

"What parolee wants to have anything to do with the police? Especially at a drinking party. I'll bet Earl was violating parole left, right and center over there tonight."

"Undoubtedly. And Vanessa," he added, glancing at her, "I'm glad you came with me tonight."

"Me, too." She smiled at him as she rubbed a cheek against the top of Tommy's head.

Shane lived on the top floor of an apartment building not far from where they had searched for Tommy. The living room was pleasantly decorated in warm earth tones nicely accented by leafy, well-placed plants. A large picture window overlooked a park and, beyond, bright city streets.

Vanessa helped Tommy out of his jacket and led him to the couch. He sat rigidly, staring at the floor, a forlorn little figure with a tear-stained face. Vanessa sat down beside him, her heart going out to him. Putting an arm around his shoulders, she drew him to her side. Shane sat beside them, concern cutting a line in his brow.

He touched the boy's shoulder gently. "Tommy—I don't like the idea of you staying with Nadine, especially with that party going on. Is there someone I can phone—your aunt or an uncle?"

Tommy's head drooped against Vanessa's shoulder. He gave it a brief shake.

"Then—would you like to stay here with me tonight?"

Tommy looked at each of them in turn. "You, too, t-teacher?" he asked with a hiccuping sob.

"This is Mr. Wilder's home, Tommy," Vanessa explained. "I live somewhere else. But you can stay here and get a good night's sleep and I'll see you in school tomorrow morning."

Tommy turned suddenly and burrowed against her shoulder, his fingers clutching her sweater. "I don't wanna stay without you."

As she held him to her, she felt his tears start anew. Dismayed, she looked at Shane.

"I think you'll have to stay, too—teacher," Shane murmured.

Her dismay deepening, Vanessa gave her head a quick shake. "I can't. You know that."

"What will it hurt?" Shane asked. "The poor kid's had all he can take these past few days. If it'll make him feel better to have you here—then why not stay?"

If there was anything but concern for Tommy behind Shane's insistence, it didn't show. Still...she knew the risks involved if others found out she'd spent the night there. She looked down at Tommy huddled now in the crook of her arm, tear-washed eyes staring up at her.

"Would it make you feel better if I stayed here, too, Tommy?" she asked.

Tommy hiccuped and nodded.

Smiling gently, she tightened her hold on him. "Then I'll stay." She looked across his head to Shane. "For Tommy," she added almost defiantly.

"I know that, Vanessa," he said as if annoyed that she would think otherwise. "It's all settled, then, Tommy. You'll both stay. Is that all right with you?"

There was a look of relief on Tommy's face as he nodded.

"Great." Shane smiled at him, squeezing his shoulder affectionately. "Now—would you like some scrambled eggs and toast?"

Tommy's eyes widened and he nodded again.

"Okay—and I think you should have a bath while I'm cooking. It'll warm you right up. Okay?"

Tommy squirmed with boyish reluctance. "I guess."

Shane laughed and ruffled the boy's hair. "It'll feel good, I promise. Come on, buddy, I'll start the water for you. I'll be back in a minute," he said to Vanessa as he and Tommy stood up. "Make yourself some coffee if you'd like."

Vanessa nodded, but she was frowning as she watched them leave the room, wishing she didn't feel so nervous about staying. She knew how much Tommy wanted her there—and it would be easier all around for Shane if she stayed. She was worried about spending the night in the same apartment as Shane. But he wouldn't try anything, would he? especially with Tommy around. If he did, he was not the man she was beginning to think he was. No, she would be safe she assured herself and picked up the phone from the table beside her and dialed.

She was hanging up when Shane came back into the room. "Who'd you call?" He sat down on the couch.

"My grandmother. I had to let her know I wouldn't be home tonight."

His eyes sparkled. "Do you always call her when you won't be home?"

She frowned darkly and glared at him. "Shane—I'm not feeling all that good about this. Don't make it worse."

He held up his hands. "Sorry." A look of concern crossed his face. "I didn't think of this before—but could you get into trouble over this?"

"I might be accused of acting in a less than professional manner, and told that I should have let the Children's Aid handle it. But—" she paused "—contacting them could create a whole lot of problems for Tommy and his mother. This is probably the best solution, for tonight anyway."

"I couldn't have left him there, Vanessa," he said quietly.

"I know. And as far as I'm concerned, you did the right thing. I think, though, that you should try to see Tommy's aunt first thing in the morning, before Nadine gets a chance."

Shane nodded thoughtfully. "I'll do that. And maybe there's some way to get word to Tommy's mother, let her know what's been going on." He looked at her and smiled crookedly. "Thanks, Vanessa."

Vanessa returned his smile. "Any time," she said lightly, suddenly aware of just how much she liked this man.

Shane stood up. "Now," he said briskly, "I'd better get into that kitchen. Tommy's ravenous. What about you?" he asked. "Could you eat?"

"Something light," she admitted, getting to her feet and following him to the kitchen. "What I'd really like is some cocoa. How's your milk situation?"

"I went shopping yesterday," he said, opening the fridge. "The cupboards are full." He handed her a carton of milk and then reached for the eggs. "There's a tin of cocoa on the shelf above the stove and the mugs are beside the sink. Just heat it in the microwave. Can you make one for each of us?" he requested as he started cracking eggs into a bowl.

"Do you do a lot of cooking?" Vanessa asked, pouring milk into mugs. "Or do you just have one or two specialties—like what you made for supper tonight?"

Shane beat the eggs with a whisk. "I cook a lot," he said. "I always have." He looked up from the frothy eggs, catching her eyes for a moment. "My mother didn't bother about food a lot," he said, his voice even, masking emotion. "I learned to cook at an early age. It was either that or go hungry."

Vanessa set the mugs in the microwave. "Is your mother still living?"

He gave an abrupt shake of his head. "She died when I was eighteen," he said without expression. "From complications due to her—alcoholism."

"I'm sorry, Shane." Vanessa's eyes were soft with sympathy.

"Yeah, well, at least I didn't have to worry about her anymore." There was a shade of pain belying the cynicism in his voice.

"What about your father?"

"My father lives in Halifax with his second wife," Shane stated flatly. "The woman he left my mother for." He poured the eggs into a frying pan sizzling with melted butter.

"When did you see him last?" Vanessa wondered just how much he would reveal to her.

"At my mother's funeral." He stirred the eggs slowly, his face tight. "He wanted me to go back with him, but I refused."

"What did you do then?"

"I got a part-time job, thanks to Uncle Henry, and a student loan to start university. Hey," he said, changing the subject, "I forgot about the toast. There's a loaf of rye bread in the bread box and the toaster's in the cupboard below. Get started on it, will you?" he ordered with a playful grin.

"Yes, sir!" Vanessa said smartly, knowing the question period was over. She watched him covertly as she sliced the bread and dropped it into the toaster. He pushed the eggs around the pan with a spatula, staring at them as though his thoughts were a thousand miles away. Tommy's situation had obviously brought back a lot of painful memories, she thought.

She had a feeling that he rarely, if ever, shared anything about his past. If it hadn't been for his concern over Tommy, it was unlikely that he would have said as much to her as he had. Shane Wilder, she was sure, was a very private man.

"The eggs are ready," he said. "How's the toast?"

"Almost done. Do you want two pieces?"

"Just one," he answered, spooning fluffy golden eggs onto plates. "I'll go see if Tommy's ready." He put the pan in the sink to soak, flashing his usual smile as he passed her. Childhood ghosts had been banished.

Vanessa put the eggs, toast and cocoa on the table in the dining area off the kitchen and sat down just as Shane came back with Tommy.

Tommy was dressed in one of Shane's sweatshirts with the sleeves rolled up, the bottom hanging halfway down his thin, pale legs. Vanessa smiled at him, smoothing damp, wiry hair back from his face.

"Sit here, Tommy," she invited, pulling out the chair beside her. "And get those eggs down while they're still hot."

Tommy sat, his head drooping until his chin almost rested against his chest. Vanessa's heart went out to him. Poor little guy, she thought, with a pang of compassion. "What's the matter?" she asked gently, touching his shoulder.

"I—I want my mom," he whispered. A fat tear glistened on his cheek.

"I know you do, sweetie." Vanessa rubbed his back soothingly. "It's been rough for you, hasn't it?" She looked up and saw the empathy on Shane's face.

"I'll see if I can phone her tomorrow, Tommy," Shane said with gruff concern.

Tommy looked up slowly. "I don't got her phone number," he said in a subdued voice.

"Well, one way or another, I'll try and get hold of her. That's a promise, buddy. And I'll make sure you don't have to go back and stay with Nadine. Okay?"

Tommy nodded, wiping a sleeve across his face. "Okay."

"Good. Eat up now," Shane commanded gently.

His fears laid to rest, at least for a while, Tommy tackled his food with gusto.

Shane spread a piece of toast with grape jelly and handed it to Tommy. "I'll make up a bed for him on the floor," he told Vanessa. "I've got some big cushions that should be comfortable." He looked at the boy with a smile. "He looks tired enough to sleep anywhere."

Tommy was slumped in his chair, slowly chewing the last of his toast, a chocolate mustache glistening on his upper lip. He blinked sleepily.

"Come on, Tommy old pal," Shane said, coming around the table and guiding him from his chair. "Curl up on the couch while I get a bed ready for you." Yawning widely, Tommy followed Shane to the couch.

Vanessa cleared away the dishes while Shane retrieved some pillows and blankets from a linen closet and arranged them in a corner of the living room. By the time he had finished, Tommy was fast asleep on the couch.

Vanessa watched from the kitchen doorway as Shane carefully picked him up and carried him across the room. Gently he laid Tommy down on the cushions and drew a sheet and then a blanket over him, tucking it in snugly. The boy murmured sleepily and then, with a sigh, settled back to sleep.

"He looks very comfortable," Vanessa said in a low voice as Shane dimmed the lights and came back into the kitchen.

"A lot more comfortable than he would have been at home with that party going on," Shane said. "Thanks for cleaning up," he added, looking around the spotless kitchen.

"You're welcome." Vanessa smiled. "This is a nice apartment," she went on. "Have you lived here long?"

"Just over a year," he answered. "I like it. It's close to everything, and quiet. I need that when I'm working."

"Speaking of working—where do you?"

"In the second bedroom. I've made it into a den of sorts, nothing fancy. Would you like to see it?"

"Yes, I would." She was curious to see where his books took shape.

There was hardly any furniture in the small room other than a large oak desk with a word processor and a few neatly stacked piles of paper on top. Above an overflowing bookcase hung several enlarged covers of his books, framed, a bright contrast to the beige walls. Vanessa looked around with avid interest.

"So this is where Matt Savage comes to life," she said, running a hand over the keyboard on the word processor. "You write the modern way, I see."

"It took some getting used to. I'd started out writing longhand—but it was worth the effort. It makes the endless editing a lot easier."

Vanessa picked up a paperback from the bookcase. "*The Case of the Purloined Pearls*," she read, examining the vivid cover. "Your first, right?"

Shane made a little gesture of dismissal. "I've improved a lot since then—along with the covers," he added with a smile. "Those first books were pretty bare—lots of mystery, but no real depth."

Vanessa glanced at the desk with its neat stacks of paper. "What's the one you're working on now about?"

"It's called *Dance with Death*. A man wants to get rid of his wife, by murdering her, of course. He kills her as she's coming out of her dance class, and then, to throw suspicion from himself, kills another woman under the same circumstances. It becomes a psychopathic obsession—he can't stop killing. Enter Matt Savage."

"Who stops him cold," Vanessa finished. "It sounds—well, gory," she added with a little grimace.

Shane chuckled at her expression. "I keep the gore to a minimum. I'm more interested in the psychological twists, the clues. That's what my readers want."

Vanessa nodded. "That's what Gran says she likes about your books." She turned over the book and skimmed the blurb on the back cover. "I have a confession to make."

Shane raised his eyebrows in query. "What?"

"I still haven't read any of your books. Yet," she added quickly.

"Is that all?" His voice dropped suggestively as his eyes took on a teasing gleam. "And here I thought you were going to confess to having an overwhelming desire to—kiss me."

Vanessa's head shot up and she stepped back. "I'm not here for that," she said sharply.

He sighed. "I know. You're here for Tommy and I'm grateful, but—" he cocked his head and smiled, dimples quivering beside his sensuous mouth. "Not even one little kiss?" His voice was low, his face only inches from hers.

"Not even one." She forced herself to relax, to try to treat his suggestion as though it was no more than a teasing remark, hoping to dispel the tension she could feel in the pit of her stomach. If the truth be known, she would love to feel the touch of his lips against hers, feel the pressure of his— She stopped the unwanted thoughts with a frown and a little shake of her head, wishing again she had suggested they take Tommy back to her place. Staying here tonight was a mistake, she thought.

Shane stood with his hands in his pockets watching the expressions flicker across her face. "Don't look so formidable," he said. "I promise to behave myself."

"Just see that you do, Mr. Wilder," Vanessa said sternly, exaggerating the tone she used to quell misbehaving students.

"Yes, Ms Evans." Shane chuckled. Still smiling, he inclined his head toward the doorway. "C'mon—let's go back to the living room. I'll fix you a drink."

"That sounds good," she said, following him out of the room and down the short hallway. "What do you have?"

"Brandy?"

"Okay, but make it small."

As Shane poured the brandy, Vanessa knelt beside the soft pile of pillows that was Tommy's bed. Smiling, she gently brushed back a lock of hair from his forehead and tucked the blanket closer around his shoulders. The boy gave a sleepy murmur, sighed, and turned onto his side. Quietly Vanessa stood up and turned around to find Shane watching her.

"He's sleeping like a baby," she assured him, flushing a little under the directness of his gaze. Crossing the room, she sat in the armchair opposite the couch.

"Good," Shane said. "Poor kid—it's been a rough few days for him." He handed Vanessa a snifter of brandy.

She smiled up at him. "Thanks."

"I've got a couple of things to do. There's some magazines on the coffee table," he said, looking over his shoulder as he left the room.

Vanessa leafed through a news magazine paying little attention to the words as she sipped her drink. She just welcomed the distraction.

Shane returned after a few minutes. "I changed the sheets on my bed," he said. "And put one of my sweat suits out for you to wear. You may have to do some sleeve rolling, but it should be comfortable enough."

Vanessa looked at him with a slight frown of dismay. "I'd rather sleep on the couch," she said. Sleeping in his bed would feel far too intimate.

"It's all arranged." Shane poured himself a brandy and flopped down on the couch, stretching his long legs out in front of him. "You'll have more privacy that way, and besides, I'm usually up late. The couch is the best place for me."

Vanessa nodded reluctantly, taking another sip of her drink and feeling unusually tense. Spending the night had seemed the right thing to do when Tommy was awake, keeping her busy with his needs. Now that he was asleep, she began questioning her decision, but there wasn't much she could do about it at this point. Taking another swallow of brandy, she determinedly pushed the feelings of uneasiness aside. She knew Shane well enough—she hoped—to be confident that he wouldn't try to take advantage of her position. Taking a final drink, she put down her empty glass.

"Can I get you another?" Shane asked.

"No, thanks." She wanted to be relaxed, not drunk. "I was under the impression you didn't drink," she said as he raised his glass to his mouth.

"I don't often," he said, eyeing the amber liquid in his glass. "I've got nothing against having the occasional drink—it's the dependency, the constant use that I object to." His lips twisted briefly. "I saw firsthand what it can do."

"It must have been rough," Vanessa said softly, picturing him as a young boy desperately trying to cope with his mother's drinking problem. "But, in my opinion, Shane, you came out of it all right."

Shane gave a short, almost scoffing laugh. "Have I? Sometimes I wonder." Frowning, he gave his head a brief shake and changed the subject. "Tell me honestly—was your grandmother upset when you told her you were spending the night? I like her," he confessed. "I'd hate to have her mad at me."

Feeling more comfortable as the brandy warmed and relaxed her, Vanessa gave a little laugh and shook her head. "Mad? Not a chance. She likes you, Shane Wilder. Besides, she understood why I felt I had to stay. I'm a little worried about Marcie, though," she added thoughtfully. "I don't want her thinking that there's more to this than there is." She looked up. "I've always tried to set a good example for her—none of this do as I say and not as I do business." She gave a rueful smile. "It isn't always easy."

"Marcie's a good kid. Smart, too," Shane said with conviction. "I think you and Cora have done a damned good job raising her. But if you think she'll misunderstand why you're staying—well, I can talk to her if you'd like."

"Thanks—we'll see how it goes. She's usually pretty understanding, but she is at a difficult age. And, Shane—I appreciate your not making any more out of this than there is. Some men would have made this very awkward."

Surprised, Shane looked at her and then shook his head with a wry smile. "Just keeping it friendly," he said dryly, swirling the brandy in his glass.

Relieved, Vanessa glanced at the clock on the wall. It was only ten-thirty but she didn't want to sit there any longer lulled by soft lights and brandy. Her attraction toward Shane had grown considerably that evening. She had found him attractive before, and had been infatuated by his charm and easy, flirtatious manner. But after tonight.... She glanced at him, her heartbeat quickening. After she'd witnessed his tender concern for Tommy, caught a glimpse of the vulnerability beneath his confident masculinity, she knew it was more than a physical thing—much more. And it made her uneasy.

"I think I'll turn in now," she said, standing up abruptly.

Shane raised his eyebrows. "Already? Well—good night. Call if you need anything."

"I'll be fine, thanks." She picked up her purse from the floor beside the chair. "Good night." She gave Shane one last look as she left the room.

Vanessa pulled on the soft, well-worn sweat suit Shane had left in the bathroom for her, tying the drawstring securely. The top was too big and the V-neck kept slipping down over one shoulder, but it would do. There was a toothbrush still in its wrapper beside the sink and she assumed it was for her. As she unwrapped it and squeezed on a dollop of minty toothpaste, she wondered if Shane kept a ready supply of toiletries for overnight guests. Women guests, she thought, wondering if he was the type to have a few long-term relationships or many short affairs. Either way, she doubted that he was ever without a woman for long.

Holding her folded clothes against herself, she opened the bathroom door slowly and looked down the hall. She could hear the murmur of the TV and hoped Shane would stay in the living room watching it.

On impulse she tiptoed across the hall to his den, flicking on the light as she went to the bookcase. Hurriedly, she pulled one of his books from the shelf. She knew sleep wouldn't come easily and if she was going to lie awake half the night, she may as well read. Besides, she thought, quietly leaving the room, it was about time she found out just what Matt Savage was all about.

Shane's bedroom was large, with elegant French doors leading to a balcony. The king-size bed was covered with a charcoal gray comforter with red stripes turned down to reveal crisp matching sheets. A chrome-plated bedside lamp softly lit the room.

Vanessa closed the door firmly behind herself, her eyes narrowing as she caught a faint whiff of Shane's musky after-shave. After putting her clothes neatly on top of one of the dressers, she sat tentatively on the edge of the bed.

She read the title of the book she'd chosen. *The Midnight Strangler.* She made a little face. It was not the type of book she usually read, having a preference for biographies, historical fiction and the occasional romance. Still, she felt a little thrill of anticipation as she opened the book and began to read Shane's words.

At first the knowledge that he had written it was distracting, but the story soon captivated her. Lying back on the fluffy pillows with the comforter tucked snugly around her, she read with growing fascination.

The characters were well-drawn and interesting. There was a poetic touch to the descriptive scenes that delighted her, and the hero was surprisingly appealing—a tall, strong man with a tough exterior that didn't always hide his heart of gold. Suspense built quickly and held.

It was after midnight when she finished the last page. Yawning widely, she put down the book and turned out the light. Sliding deep under the covers, she curled up on her side and smiled into the darkness. Add another fan to your list, Shane Wilder, she thought sleepily.

THE SUN WAS GLIMMERING in the eastern sky when Shane woke up. He looked at Tommy, still snuggled into his nest of pillows, nothing visible but his shock of reddish hair. Moving quietly to the bathroom, Shane shaved and showered, then quickly dressed. He carefully opened the door to his bedroom, and crossed the floor to stand beside his bed, looking down on the sleeping woman.

She lay on her stomach with one arm dangling over the edge of the bed, her face partially covered by a lock of golden-brown hair.

He knelt and picked up her hand, holding it in his. "Vanessa," he said softly. There was no response. He tightened his hand on hers and tried again. "Vanessa," he repeated, his voice a loud whisper.

Her answer was a muffled groan. "Come on, Vanessa," he coaxed. "It's time to get up."

One green-flecked eye opened and looked blurrily at him. "Go away," she muttered, pulling her hand from his and burrowing deeper under the covers.

"Coffee's on." Shane chuckled. "I can set up an IV if you want to mainline it."

Vanessa stuck out an arm. "Lots of milk, no sugar," she mumbled, eyes still closed.

Laughing, Shane pushed up the sleeve and stroked the silky skin of her inner arm. "Are you always this cranky in the morning?"

This time both eyes flicked open. "Only when people insist on talking to me." She blinked groggily. "What time is it?"

"Seven-thirty. There's enough time for you to shower and have a bite to eat."

Vanessa pushed herself to a sitting position, pulling up the neckline of the sweatshirt as it slipped over one shoulder. "I'll go home to shower. I need to change my clothes for school."

"Then I'll drive you as soon as Tommy's ready."

She shook her head, pushing the hair back from her face. "Let him sleep as long as possible. The poor little guy is worn out. I'll take a cab."

"Are you sure?"

"Yes," she nodded. "It'll be easier all around." She stretched lazily and yawned. "Where's that coffee?"

"In the kitchen," Shane said, remaining where he was. "You know, Vanessa, cranky or not, you look beautiful in the morning." He took her hand and stroked her fingers. "Lying on my bed, all soft and warm...temptingly cuddly." He raised her hand to his mouth and kissed the palm lightly, his eyes dancing at the flash of consternation on her face.

"Shane—" Vanessa pulled her hand away and tried to look severe. "Behave yourself," she admonished. "I was just beginning to think you were a gentleman, after all." Inside her pulse was fluttering and a soft smile was threatening to break out. "Please let me get up—I need that coffee."

"Yes, ma'am." Shane smiled in lazy amusement as he straightened and went out of the room.

What an incredibly sexy man, Vanessa thought as she swung her feet to the floor, wondering how long she would be able to resist him if he ever decided to make a real play. All of five minutes, she acknowledged ruefully as she picked up her clothes and went to the bathroom. Keeping their relationship on a friendship level, she had to admit, would depend almost entirely on him, and that made her feel decidedly uneasy.

She pulled on her jeans and sweatshirt after a quick wash. She folded Shane's sweat suit neatly, and went into the living room. Shane had already put away the blankets he had used and had left a cup of coffee for her on the table in the dining area. He was kneeling beside Tommy, gently waking him.

"Come on, Tom," he said, giving the boy's thin little shoulders a squeeze. "It's time to get up. Breakfast is ready."

Blinking rapidly, Tommy looked around in confusion for a second and then, sitting up, he grinned widely, his pale blue eyes crinkling at the corners. "I'm hungry," he told Shane.

"Good. I made a big pot of oatmeal with raisins and brown sugar to put on it. You go get washed and dressed while I dish it out."

Tommy nodded and scampered up off the pillows, heading for the bathroom.

Vanessa watched, sipping her coffee, admiring the tenderness with which Shane treated Tommy. It added a dimension to his masculinity that she found tremendously appealing.

Shane came out of the kitchen with two bowls of oatmeal. "Want some?" he asked Vanessa.

She shook her head quickly, suppressing a shudder. "I'll phone for a cab now," she said. "I don't think I could survive watching you two eat that stuff. Mornings make me nauseated."

Shane chuckled as he set the steaming bowls on placemats. "I'll phone for you in a minute," he said. "Finish your coffee." He sat down and took a sip of orange juice. "Now—I'm going to drive Tommy to school and then try to see his aunt in the hospital. I'm sure I can convince the hospital authorities to let me see her outside of visiting hours under the circumstances."

Vanessa nodded. "I think maybe you should talk to Bettina before you go. It might be more reassuring to Tommy's aunt if Bettina called her first to let her know that you're connected with the school. Also," she added, picking up her cup, "you can explain to Bettina why I'm late, which I'm going to be. Only Bettina, though," she cautioned quickly. "I don't want any of the others speculating about—about why I spent the night here."

"Don't worry," Shane said, grinning at her. "Your reputation is safe with me."

Vanessa looked away from his laughing eyes and took a sip of coffee. But am I? she wondered, feeling again that twinge of emotion.

"THAT WAS QUITE A STORY Shane told me earlier," Bettina said, sitting behind her desk and leaning back in her chair. "I'd like to hear your side of it now."

"Right." Vanessa quickly relayed to Bettina the events of the previous night. "And I stayed because it made Tommy feel better to have me there," she finished.

Bettina was nodding, her black eyes thoughtful. "You know, Vanessa," she said, "that professionally I have to tell you that you should have let the authorities handle this. But, personally, I think you and Shane did the right thing. The boy was frightened, tired. And you did what was best for him. I know Tommy's mother. She's a good woman, trying hard to make things work for herself and Tommy. I would have hated for her to become involved in a dispute over Tommy's well-being, through no fault of her own. You know how embroiled these things can become." Her eyes sparkled suddenly and she grinned. "So—how was it?"

"How was what?"

"Spending the night with Shane."

"Bettina!" Vanessa frowned. "It was strictly for Tommy—Shane slept on the couch."

Bettina raised her eyebrows. "Not even a little kiss and cuddle?"

"No, Bettina. Nothing like that at all."

"Is that disappointment I hear in your voice?"

Vanessa laughed lightly and shrugged. "Not really. I'll admit that I probably wouldn't have resisted a good-night kiss." She looked away self-consciously. "Who would? But—he's not the man for me, Bettina, not in the long run. You know I can't handle short-term relationships, and from what I've come to know about him, short term is all he's looking for. A—a dalliance." She looked down at her hands. "He tempts me . . . but he'll also hurt me, intentionally or not."

"Well, you know what's best for yourself," Bettina said, her smile soft and sympathetic. "But don't be too quick to shut him out, Van. He's quite a man."

Vanessa looked up with a little smile. "He is, isn't he?"

"Oh, by the way," Bettina went on, "he asked me to give you a message. He wants you to meet him at Echo's for lunch so he can fill you in on his visit to the hospital. I told him you would be there just after twelve. Okay?"

Vanessa nodded. "Okay." Already she was looking forward to seeing him again.

The interior of Echo's was dimly lit. Vanessa blinked her eyes, adjusting from the bright sunlight, as she hung up her coat and followed the hostess to the table where Shane was waiting. She was conscious of his narrow-eyed scrutiny as she approached. Smiling and a little breathless, she sat down.

"Hi," she said.

"Hi, yourself," he returned, his eyes still fixed on hers.

"Stop staring," she demanded after an uncomfortable moment.

He smiled lazily, his dimples quivering in his lean face. "I was just trying to decide," he said, his voice low and intimate as he put his arms on the table and leaned closer, "when it is you look the sexiest." Vanessa felt uncomfortable with the direction the conversation was taking.

"You were a knockout in those tight black jeans last night. And this morning, you were absolutely delectable when you woke up in my bed all soft and warm." His teeth flashed in a wide grin as the color rose in her face. "And now," he continued, "you're beautiful, with your hair up and little wisps curling around your face." He reached across the table and ran a finger from her chin over her throat to lightly touch the lace that peeped above the top button of her blouse.

"Vanessa Evans, you are one hell of an attractive woman." He dropped his hand to cover hers where it lay on the table.

Vanessa pulled her hand quickly away, forcing a look of mock severity on her flushed face. "Please, Shane," she said. "I didn't come here to flirt with you."

He sighed with disappointment. "No?"

"No," she said firmly. "I came to find out what you've managed to do about Tommy this morning."

"Let's order first," he suggested. "Then I'll fill you in."

"Good. I'm starving." She looked quickly at the menu and then closed it. "I'm going to have the chef's salad."

"You're starving and you'll settle for a salad? Are you dieting?"

"No, but I try to be reasonable so I won't have to. I'm getting to the age when things could start to expand." She puffed out her cheeks.

Shane chuckled. "What age is that?"

"Twenty-eight."

He looked surprised. "Really? I would have thought you were younger."

Vanessa laughed. "I'm also getting to the age when I appreciate hearing that. How old are you, by the way?"

"Thirty-three. Not too old for you, am I?"

She shook her head. "Too young. I prefer older men, gray haired and distinguished looking." She smiled at him and then glanced at her watch. "We'd better order. I have to be back by one—I've got a class first thing."

"Right." Shane signaled to the waiter. "Would you like a glass of wine with your meal?"

She shook her head. "No, thank you. It'll just make me sleepy."

Vanessa ordered and watched Shane as he placed his order. He's so handsome, she thought, and so—likable. She might find the strength to resist a purely physical attraction, but... She sighed, fiddling with her fork, wishing she could relax and give in to the attraction she felt for him, let it lead where it may, consequences be damned.

"You look pensive," Shane stated as the waiter departed with their orders.

"Just thinking about Tommy," she said quickly. "What happened this morning?"

"Well, after I spoke to Bettina," he began, "I went to the hospital and managed to see Alma without too much trouble. She's Tommy's aunt on his father's side. A very nice woman, by the way. Anyway, her angina acted up. A bad attack. Nadine just happened to be visiting when it all happened, so Alma asked her to stay with Tommy."

"Doesn't she know what Nadine is like?"

"Alma put the blame on Earl and his friends. She was quite upset when she heard he was out of jail. It seems Nadine really isn't all that bad, except when Earl is around. Then she starts drinking and, well, we saw where that led."

Vanessa grimaced and nodded. "So—what's going to happen to Tommy?"

"Tommy's mother will be back on Monday. We managed to phone her and she gave permission for Tommy to stay with me until she gets back."

"That's great, Shane!"

"Yeah." He smiled with satisfaction. "I really like the boy, Vanessa. It'll be great having him around for a while. Oh—and Alma also gave me permission to evict Nadine and Earl."

"Did you?"

"Damned right I did." Shane was silent as the waiter served them.

"Go on," Vanessa urged as soon as the waiter had departed. "What happened?"

"It was quite easy, really," Shane said, picking up half of his Rueben sandwich. "I rousted them out of bed and told them they had half an hour to clear out or our friend Sergeant Preston would be called in to investigate." He took a bite of his sandwich.

"Did they give you any trouble?" Vanessa asked, picking at her salad.

Shane swallowed and shook his head. "There was a bit of profanity and protest, but they were both too hung over to be any real problem. Besides, I told Earl that it was only fair to warn him that I was an expert in martial arts and that if he tried anything I'd break his face. Then I strutted around looking as though I was itching to do just that."

Vanessa laughed. "And are you? An expert in martial arts?"

"Nope. I was hoping that like most bullies he was also a coward."

Vanessa looked at him with a smile of admiration. "Way to go, Shane Wilder. Have you told Tommy yet?"

"Not yet. I'll go back with you to the school and tell him. You know, Vanessa," he went on, "I'm going to have to keep him entertained all weekend."

Vanessa nodded. "So?"

"So maybe I'll need some help. I'm not used to having a kid around. You're surrounded by them all day long. You know what they like doing."

She looked at him suspiciously. "Are you working on a ploy to get me to go out with you?"

Shane looked at her in mock surprise. "Of course not. I have only Tommy's best interests at heart. As my—friend—surely you'll help?"

Vanessa raised her hands in a gesture of defeat and smiled helplessly. "I'll help."

"Good," Shane said with evident satisfaction.

Vanessa nibbled on a piece of cheese, hoping she wasn't headed straight for trouble. "Oh, by the way," she said suddenly. "I read one of your books last night—*The Midnight Strangler*."

"I noticed it in my room," Shane said. "So?" He looked as though he was prepared for criticism.

She grinned widely. "I liked it—very much. You're a good writer, Shane. There was one thing, though."

"What was that?"

"Why did Matt have to walk away from Monica at the end? I liked her—they would have been good together."

"Matt knows he's not the marrying kind," Shane explained. "He leaves 'em before he hurts 'em."

"It sounds like a motto," Vanessa said, making a face. "Does that mean a different woman in each book?"

"So far. And I'll probably keep it that way."

"That's too bad. I like romantic endings." After coffee and dessert Vanessa glanced at her watch. "I have to get back. Did you say you were coming to talk to Tommy?"

"I am. Need a ride?"

"Yes, please. And thanks for lunch."

"You're welcome—but you'll be earning it over the next few days, helping me with Tommy." He smiled as he held her coat for her.

"Oh, yeah?" she asked, sliding her arms into her coat. She turned to look at him. "And just what is it you've got planned?"

"A little bit of everything." He grinned. "Just wait and see."

As Vanessa stood by the door waiting for Shane to pay the check, a petite woman with a wild mane of red hair and a gauzy black dress came up to Shane and laid a hand on his arm. Shane turned, his expression one of pleasure as he took the woman's hand in his, holding it as he leaned forward to catch what she was saying. He grinned and said something that caused the woman to toss her head back and laugh in high-pitched tones. They spoke for another moment before he bent to drop a quick kiss on her cheek and then stood watching as she strode back to her table.

Vanessa could see the look of appreciation lighting his face and hid a grimace as he turned and made his way to her.

"Sorry about that," he said with a smile. "That was Corrine Carriere—the actress. She's on lunch break from rehearsing a play at the Theater Center. She's an old friend," he added, pushing open the door.

Vanessa merely smiled and nodded as she followed Shane to his car. As she got in, she wondered just how many other "old friends" there were in Shane's life and if, someday, he'd use those words to describe her.

"Better hurry," she said as Shane got in and started the engine. "Bell rings in five minutes." She smiled at him and wished, not for the first time, that he was just a little less attractive.

CHAPTER FIVE

"AUNT VAN—PHONE." Marcie poked her head into Vanessa's room. "Aunt Van?"

Vanessa rolled over in bed and opened her eyes, blinking sleepily. "What?" she mumbled.

"Phone," Marcie repeated patiently, accustomed to her aunt's morning vagueness. "It's Shane. Are you awake?"

"Almost. Thanks." Yawning, she reached for the phone beside her bed. "Hello."

"Vanessa?" Shane's voice was low and intimate. "Don't tell me I woke you up."

"Okay, I won't tell you." Vanessa lay back on the pillow, cradling the phone between her ear and shoulder.

"Are you all set to help me with Tommy today?"

"I helped you last night. I sat through two *Star Wars* tapes and made three bowls of popcorn."

"And wasn't it fun?" Shane laughed. "Listen—I've got a great idea for today."

"What is it this time—Space Invaders at the arcade?"

"Much better. Do you skate?"

"Doesn't every true Canadian?"

"Then dust off the old skate blades—we're going skating today. Marcie, too, if she wants to come along."

"All right. I guess I can make it—for Tommy's sake." Vanessa's voice sounded sleepily resigned, but she was pleased. Being with Shane is so much fun, she thought, smiling. "Where and when?" she asked him.

"Where is a surprise. When depends on how fast you can get yourself out of bed."

Vanessa snuggled a little deeper under the covers and moaned softly.

"Lazy lady," he teased. "You're missing the best part of the day."

"You sound just like Gran and Marcie do in the morning. Disgustingly cheerful."

Shane chuckled. "And you sound cranky. When are you planning to get up?"

She stifled a yawn. "Soon, I suppose."

"Good. I'll pick you up at noon. Tommy's itching for some physical activity."

"Noon sounds fine, Shane. I don't move very fast on Sundays. That should give me enough time to put myself together."

"I'll provide lunch. And one more thing, Vanessa..."

She could hear laughter in his voice. "What?"

"Do you sleep in the nude?"

"What? That's none of your business, Mr. Wilder," Vanessa said in her best schoolteacher's voice, but she could feel a warm flush suffuse her cheeks. "I'll see you later. That is," she admonished with mock severity, "if you promise to behave yourself."

He sighed. "All right, I promise. I don't think I've ever behaved myself as much as I have the past few days."

That was probably true, Vanessa mused. "It's good for you," she told him. "Bye now." She hung up and rolled over, smiling softly. Her weekend had been spent almost entirely with Shane, and Tommy, of course. It had been fun. When had she last laughed as much as she had during the past few days? Shane made her feel good. She enjoyed his company tremendously.

She stretched her long legs, feeling the mattress roll gently under her, grimacing as she acknowledged that she wasn't the only woman who enjoyed his company. The night before, while watching the *Star Wars* movies at his place, the phone had rung. Automatically, she had reached to answer it.

"Leave it," Shane had said. "I've got the answering machine on."

The phone stopped ringing and after a beep, a woman's voice, low and sultry, sounded in the room.

"Shane, I'm sorry about how I reacted when you cancelled our date for tonight. It's just—" she sighed "—I was so disappointed. I'm sure the little boy is charming." The voice dropped suggestively. "I promise I'll make it up to you, darling. Call me. Bye bye."

Vanessa swung her legs out of bed, scowling at the memory of the woman's voice. Shane hadn't said anything; he just listened with a frown and a slight shake of his head, as if the woman had displeased him. Who was she? Just one of the many woman he knew, Vanessa thought, tying her bathrobe around her waist as she headed for the bathroom. And there had to be a lot of women in his life. He'd attract them like a magnet, she thought, with his charm and good looks.

Vanessa knew how little resistance she herself had to his seductiveness and wondered again how wise it was to be seeing so much of him. She couldn't lie to herself and pretend this weekend had been just for Tommy. As much as she liked the boy and was concerned for his well-being, she was falling in with Shane's plans mainly because she wanted to see Shane.

So far he had treated her in a friendly, undemanding manner. But it wouldn't last. Vanessa knew that with certainty. She had seen desire flicker in his heavy-lidded eyes when they rested on her. He was waiting, playing it her way for now. With a little shiver of apprehension, she wondered what lay in store for her with Shane. It wasn't that she was afraid of liking him, or even of desiring him. She was afraid of loving him.

After a quick shower, Vanessa went down to the kitchen. Cora and Marcie were eating breakfast while sharing the Sunday paper.

"Morning," Marcie mumbled around a mouthful of toast.

"Good morning," Vanessa said, pouring herself a cup of coffee.

"Good morning, dear." Cora looked up from the paper. "Was that Shane on the phone?"

Vanessa nodded, sipping her coffee as she leaned back against the countertop. "He wants to take Tommy skating today. You, too, Marcie. Got any plans?"

"A bit of homework, but I'd like to go—I haven't been skating yet this year. Where are we going?"

"I don't know. One of the arenas, I guess." Vanessa reached for the coffeepot and refilled her mug. "He'll be here about noon—oh, and he's supplying lunch."

"You've seen a lot of him these last few days," Cora commented, looking at Vanessa over her glasses.

"Yes, well—he wants me to help him entertain Tommy."

"I would think a man like Shane would have very little trouble entertaining an eight-year-old boy. I think it's just an excuse."

"Maybe it is, Gran," Vanessa agreed easily. "But that doesn't mean things are going to get, well, serious between us." She frowned into her coffee. "Shane Wilder is a—ladies' man, Gran. Surely you can see that. And I'm—I'm—"

"A one-man woman," Cora finished for her. "I know that, dear, but—"

"But nothing, Gran," Vanessa interrupted firmly, knowing her grandmother's romantic bent of mind. The last thing she needed was for Cora to get the wrong idea about why she and Shane were spending so much time together. "Do you know where the skates are?" she asked her niece, changing the subject.

"In the basement, hanging up in the storage room under the stairs." Marcie looked up from the comic page, a hesitant look in her hazel eyes. "Aunt Vanessa—can I ask you something sort of personal?"

"Of course, sweetie." Vanessa had a pretty good idea what was on Marcie's mind.

Marcie's thick, dark lashes swept down and she rubbed a finger along the edge of the table. "The other night, when you—when you didn't come home..." Her voice trailed off and she looked at her aunt with concern.

"I stayed at Shane's," Vanessa explained calmly, "because of Tommy. For no other reason. He was very upset, the poor child. It seemed to make him feel better to have me there. I suppose I could have brought him here, but he'd had enough activity for one night." She smiled and added. "In case you're wondering, Shane slept on the couch, with Tommy on the floor just a few feet away. Okay?"

"Okay." Marcie nodded. "I wouldn't have minded or anything, you know. I mean, I'm old enough to understand these things."

"I know you are, Marcie," Vanessa said, sharing a quick smile with Cora. "But if I spend the night with a man, it will be because I'm in love with him and we're ready to make a commitment to each other."

"There's some very good advice in what your aunt just said," Cora interjected quietly.

"Wait for love. I know," Marcie said. "It's a good idea. I know a couple of girls who have already—you know." She frowned thoughtfully. "I don't think they're very happy about it all, no matter what they say." She looked up and grinned. "Don't worry, you two. I can wait."

But can I? Vanessa wondered a bit glumly.

SHE DRESSED IN JEANS, pulling a yellow sweatshirt over a blue-and-yellow plaid blouse. Her hair was loose, curling softly over her shoulders, and she added a green mohair beret that matched the sweater jacket she planned to wear, one that Cora had knitted for her last year.

"Are you ready?" she asked Marcie, coming into the living room to stand by the window overlooking the street.

"Yep." Marcie looked up from the book she was reading. "The skates are by the door, and I thought I'd bring my hockey stick along."

"What are you going to do today, Gran?" Vanessa turned to Cora. "You know Shane wouldn't mind if you joined us."

Cora shook her head. "I'm too old to skate, and I don't relish the idea of sitting around in the cold waiting for you to finish. I think I'll take a taxi over to Ida Corbett's this afternoon. She gets so lonely since Herbert died. Will you be home for supper?"

"I don't know. Probably. Don't bother starting anything, though, if you're home first. I'll whip something up when we get back." She saw Shane's car pull up in front of the house. "Shane's here, Marcie."

Marcie put down her book and stood up quickly, sliding her arms into her bright red ski jacket. "See you later, Gran." She grinned as she went out to the hallway to collect the skates and hockey stick. "I'll take these out to the car, Aunt Van," she called, opening the front door.

Vanessa put on her sweater and zipped it up, adjusting the big, rolled collar under her chin. "See you later, Gran. Say hello to Mrs. Corbett for me."

"Will do. Have fun, dear. Oh—do you have your house key?"

"Right here." Vanessa held up her hand, key chain dangling between her fingers. "Bye now." She waved and left.

Shane was putting the skates and hockey stick in the trunk when Vanessa came out. Marcie sat in the back of the car with Tommy.

"Hi," Shane said, slamming the trunk shut.

"Hi," Vanessa responded cheerfully. She took a deep breath and looked around. "Isn't it a beautiful day?"

"It certainly is," Shane agreed, but he was watching her, a gleam of appreciation in his clear gray eyes. He removed his car keys from the lock in the trunk and came to stand beside her. "You're very beautiful yourself, Vanessa," he murmured, running a finger softly across her lips.

"Thank you." Vanessa smiled a little nervously. Opening the car door, she slid in quickly. "Let's go," she said.

A smile played across his lips. "Right."

"Where are we going?" Vanessa asked a few minutes later after greeting Tommy and admiring the Winnipeg Jets hockey sweater Shane had bought for him. "To one of the arenas?"

Shane shook his head. "Some place much better. I've been waiting for weeks for the weather to get cold enough."

"It's outdoors, then."

"Yeah."

Vanessa gave him an exasperated look. "Is that all you're going to say?"

"Yeah," he said again, turning to grin at her. "Except wait and see."

Vanessa settled back to enjoy the ride through the city and finally out of it. It was a glorious late fall day. Barren trees displayed their stark branches against a backdrop of brilliant blue. Frost trimmed the stretching furrows of black prairie soil bordering the highway.

About ten minutes outside the city limits, Shane turned onto a gravel driveway lined with magnificent oak trees.

"Are we going to visit a friend of yours?" Vanessa asked, catching a glimpse of a house through the trees.

"Nope. We're going skating."

The house came into full view as the car rounded a curve. "Then who belongs to this?" Vanessa asked, gesturing.

"I do."

"This house is yours? Shane—it's incredible!" Vanessa leaned forward, looking around eagerly. The house was old, with gabled roof and diamond-shaped leaded-glass window panes that gleamed in the sunlight. A frozen creek, marsh grasses thick along its edge, lay at the bottom of a gently sloping hill to the back of the house.

Shane parked the car. "All out," he said.

Vanessa got out quickly, pulling her seat forward for Tommy to slip out from the back of the car. She took a deep breath of frosty, clear air and looked around with pleasure. The sun was bright in the cloudless sky and trees cast shadows across the faded lawn.

"Why don't you live here, Shane?" she asked. "It's beautiful."

Shane was beside her, looking around with obvious pride. "It is beautiful, isn't it? I plan on moving here, soon, I hope. I've been working on the house, doing some renovations—modernizing, mainly." He turned to Tommy, handing him the car keys. "Could you get the skates out of the trunk, please, Tommy?" he asked. "And Marcie, there's a bag of groceries in there as well. Could you bring it into the house for me?"

"Sure," Marcie said with her easy grin. "This is a great place, Shane."

"Thanks." Shane smiled and turning back to Vanessa, took her by the arm. "Come on. Let's go open up."

"I've been working on the kitchen," Shane explained as they entered through the back door. "It's all done except for the finishing touches. And the appliances, of course. I'm keeping that old fridge and stove here until I'm ready to move in."

Vanessa ran a hand over the new oak cabinets. "Are you doing the work yourself?"

"Some," Shane admitted. "I hired someone for the cabinets and the wiring, but I did most of the plumbing and all of the general repairs."

Vanessa looked at him with a cheeky grin. "Aren't you talented," she marveled. "And I thought all you could do was write gory books."

"You haven't seen half my talents yet, lady," he drawled with a suggestive wink.

Vanessa made a face at him and walked toward the kitchen door. "Stop flirting, Shane Wilder, and show me the rest of the house."

"Yes, ma'am." Shane followed her out of the room.

Off the kitchen was a dining area with an archway to the living room, which overlooked a wild and tangled frost-covered garden and the creek beyond. Sunlight streamed in through two floor-to-ceiling picture windows on each side of a stone fireplace, bringing out the rich dark-gold color of the oak floor and paneling. The room was unfurnished except for a threadbare strip of carpeting in front of the hearth. Vanessa opened oak-framed French doors at one end of the room and peered through.

"Oh, this is nice," she exclaimed, opening the doors wider. The adjoining room was a smaller version of the living area, with a scaled-down fireplace and the same south-easterly view. The walls were lined with built-in bookcases glowing gold in the sun-filled room.

"This will be my den," Shane said, coming up behind her. "I'm going to enjoy working in here."

"How long have you had this place?" Vanessa asked.

"A couple of years now," Shane answered. He added, "Do you remember me telling you about my Uncle Henry? Well, this was his place. He built it for his fiancée who was supposed to join him from England, but she never showed. Ran off with another man. His sister—my grandmother—came instead and lived with him for a while, but after she got married, he lived here by himself."

"Did he leave it to you?"

"He wanted to, but after he got sick he needed money. I bought it from him then."

"You're lucky to have it." Vanessa stood at one of the windows looking out on Marcie and Tommy as they explored the grounds.

"I know." Shane stood beside her, hands in the pockets of his jeans. "Uncle Henry loved this place. He didn't want it sold to someone who would tear it down and divide the land into lots for development—there are fifteen acres surrounding the house. He knew I'd want to keep it all for myself. He let me have it for a fraction of what it's really worth."

It would make a beautiful home, Vanessa thought, a perfect place to raise a family. There was lots of room for children, dogs and horses. She stole a sidelong glance at Shane as he gazed pensively out the window. Would he ever fall in love and marry, bringing a wife into this house? She had serious doubts. From all he had said, it was likely the house would remain a bachelor's haven. What a waste, she thought, looking around the room again, then back to Shane and his strong, handsome profile.

"Can we take a quick look upstairs?" she suggested, moving away from the window toward the door.

There were four bedrooms on the second floor, all good sized with gabled windows and sloping ceilings. Vanessa preferred this kind of room over the typical square-box style. All were unfurnished except for an old mattress on the floor in the master bedroom.

"The place was fully furnished when I bought it," Shane explained as they went back downstairs. "I've kept almost everything—there's a beautiful old dining-room set. I had it all put into storage until I'm ready to move in. So far, I've just spent the occasional weekend."

"When do you think you'll be moving?"

He shrugged. "By spring, I hope. I want to get the rooms painted first." He opened the door leading out to the garden. "Well?" he asked. "Are you ready to skate?"

Vanessa grinned. "You bet."

Marcie was kneeling before a wooden bench near the creek lacing up Tommy's skates. She looked up and waved as Shane and Vanessa came out of the house. "Your skates are down here," the girl called.

Shane answered with a wave of his hand as they made their way down the hill. "The creek floods in the spring," he told Vanessa, glancing at her over his shoulder. "So Henry had some landscaping done around the bank and had the house built higher than flood level, then planted trees and shrubs to give the setting a natural look.''

The whole area did have a lovely, unplanned, rugged look. Vanessa sat on the bench beside Tommy and looked around in appreciation. Cattails and red willow bushes lined the creek. Oak and ash trees studded the bank, their fallen leaves curling crisply on the golden grass, adding a dry, autumn smell to the frosty air.

"I'm going to light a fire," Shane said, indicating a stone fire pit close by. "I thought we could have a wiener roast later on."

"Did you bring marshmallows?" Marcie asked hopefully, looking up from tying her skates.

"Of course I did," Shane answered. "What's a wiener roast without marshmallows for dessert—right, Tommy?"

Tommy grinned up at Shane and nodded vigorously, causing Vanessa to smile as she pulled on a skate. It was obvious that Tommy would agree to anything Shane said.

"Ready, Tommy?" Marcie asked, standing up.

Tommy nodded again, uncertainly this time. "I don't skate too much," he confessed, with a worried look.

"That's okay," Marcie said cheerfully. "You can hang on to me if you want." She held out her hand and guided the boy onto the ice. His steps were tentative and unsteady, and he clung tightly to Marcie's hand as she skated slowly toward the middle of the creek.

"Are you sure it's safe?" Vanessa asked suddenly.

"It's safe," Shane assured her, glancing up from the fire he had started. "The creek isn't very deep anyway—all you'd get is a skate full of water if you did fall through." He tossed some wood on the fire and stood up, wiping his hands on his jeans. "Marcie's very good with Tommy," he commented, coming to sit on the bench beside her.

"She likes to be with kids—she's always baby-sitting. It comes from being an only child, I guess."

"Don't you ever have the urge to supply her with all kinds of little cousins?" Shane asked, a teasing light in his gray eyes.

"Very much so," Vanessa answered, pulling a skate lace tight. "Unfortunately I can't do it all by myself."

"A lot of women do these days," he said, pulling off his boots and reaching for his skates.

Vanessa stretched her legs out in front of her and flexed her ankles. "But I'm not one of them. I want my children to have a full-time father, not just a name on a birth certificate."

"And you'll all live happily ever after in a rose-covered cottage with a white picket fence," Shane added sardonically.

"With a little bit of luck and a lot of love, yes." Vanessa stood up and smiled. "It does happen, you know, Shane Wilder," she said with firm conviction. Stepping onto the ice, she skated gracefully away.

"Let's give Tommy a ride," she suggested to Marcie, stopping sharply beside them with a little spray of ice. "Want to go fast, Tommy?"

"Okay." Tommy grinned with enthusiasm.

"I'll take one hand and Marcie the other," she explained, taking his gloved hand in hers. "Don't worry, we'll hang on tight. You won't fall. Ready now?"

Tommy nodded, his fingers curling tightly over hers.

"Then let's go!" Laughing, she and Marcie began gliding over the ice, pulling Tommy between them. "Bend your knees a bit, Tommy—that's it! Having fun?"

"Yeah!"

"Want to go faster?"

Tommy bent his knees a little more and hung on tighter. "Yeah!"

"Then let's go, Marcie." Vanessa laughed. "Let's give him a real ride!"

Vanessa loved the swift gliding motion, the sound of the skate blades scraping against the ice. She loved the rush of air against her face, tingling cold and smelling of wood smoke. She glanced down at Tommy, his eyes narrowed and his face split by a grin.

"Let's turn here," she called to Marcie, easing into a slow curve, careful of Tommy's balance. As they straightened out again and began to skate back, she asked Tommy, "Shall we go fast again?"

Tommy risked a quick look at her. "Yeah!"

They rushed up to where Shane was stepping out onto the ice and stopped abruptly.

"I haven't done that in years." Vanessa laughed, her eyes sparkling. "Did you like it, Tommy?"

Tommy nodded. "We went fast," he told Shane.

"You sure did, buddy." Shane grinned at him. "Just like you were flying."

Tommy nodded again. "Like a hawk," he said happily.

Marcie grabbed the hockey sticks, which were propped against the trunk of an ash tree, and pulled a puck from her jacket pocket. "Here," she said, handing Tommy the shorter stick. "Let's shoot the puck around."

Tommy clutched the stick and, ankles wobbling, skated slowly behind Marcie to the center of the creek.

"He's having fun," Shane said with satisfaction.

"He is." Vanessa smiled at him. "This was a great idea, Shane. It's such a beautiful day." She pushed away slowly, doing a short turn on the point of one skate. "And it's so much fun to skate outside instead of in an arena."

"It is, isn't it?" Shane agreed. "We can come again, as long as the snow holds off." He skated up to her. "Let's go down the creek," he suggested. "It's too much for Tommy, but he's having fun with Marcie." Marcie had put two pieces of wood on the ice near the far bank and they were shooting the puck between them.

"All right." Vanessa dug her blades into the ice and pushed off quickly. "Race you," she called over her shoulder.

"Hey—you cheated." Shane skated after her, his long, deceptively lazy strides catching up to her in no time. Coming up behind her, he put his hands on her waist. "Relax," he said as she stiffened in surprise. "I'll give you a ride."

He carried them both forward with ease. Vanessa relaxed, lifting her face to feel the wind rushing past. The creek wound in slow, lazy curves through thick stands of willow, narrowing at times to little more than a trail of ice, widening suddenly to pond size and dotted with black water-worn stumps of long-dead trees.

"Let's sit for a few minutes," Shane suggested, his mouth close to her ear. He pushed them to a tree uprooted by some long-ago flood.

"That was fun." Vanessa sat on the smooth log, smiling. "Thanks for the ride."

"You're welcome." His smile was warm as he sat beside her, his shoulder pressed comfortably against hers as they sat in companionable silence.

A nuthatch walked down the gnarled trunk of an ancient peach-leaf willow searching for insects hibernating in the thick, rough bark. A breeze stirred cattails and rustled among the dry golden marsh grasses. Blue jays flew in raucous flight through the poplar trees on the slope of the far bank.

"Do you see many animals?" Vanessa asked.

"There are quite a few deer," Shane answered. "And I've seen the occasional fox. There are also lots of muskrat, beaver, raccoons and, of course, skunks. Quite enough for someone who was born and raised in the city."

"You're lucky to have this, Shane."

"I know," he agreed readily. "Just one of the many things for which I'm grateful to Henry."

"You still miss him, don't you."

"Very much so. He was a good friend."

"Like you are to Tommy. This week has done wonders for him, Shane. He seems so much more confident, less shy than he was."

"What about us, Vanessa?" he asked suddenly. "Are we friends?"

Vanessa looked down, scraping the ice with a skate blade nervously. "Yes," she said slowly. "Of course we're friends."

"That's not enough for me, Vanessa."

Surprised, Vanessa raised her head and looked at him, consternation showing plainly in her green-flecked eyes. "What?"

His eyes narrowed and held hers. "I said that's not enough for me. I want more. I want to be your lover."

Startled by the words and the intensity of his voice, Vanessa stared at him, feeling a sharp stab of excitement in her stomach. "Shane, I—"

"I know. You just want to be friends." He cupped her chin in his hand. "But Vanessa—friends can become lovers." Slowly, his eyes holding hers, he lowered his head, his lips barely touching hers. "Don't you agree?" His voice was a deep whisper.

She braced herself to resist passion, but his lips touched hers with a warm tenderness that was her undoing. With a sigh, she gave herself to his kiss, savoring the soft heat of his mouth, kissing him back with a desire that grew in slow, delicious waves.

"Mm," murmured Shane, pulling back. "That was worth waiting for." He ran a finger down the curve of her flushed cheek. "I like being friends with you, Vanessa Evans." He stood up and held out a hand to her. "Let's get back to the kids," he said. "And the hot dogs. I'm hungry."

Vanessa put her hand in his and let him pull her to her feet, wondering just how much strength her legs had left. His kiss had left her feeling weak, shaken.

They skated back slowly. Vanessa left her hand in his, a rueful smile playing on her lips. It had been a perfect first kiss, she decided, neither tentative nor demanding, enticing response, not rebuff. It would be hard, she knew, to refuse him another.

She glanced at him, her smile turning suddenly into a frown. He wanted to sleep with her—he made no pretense about it. But he wasn't storming her with passion, as if he knew that would only strengthen her resistance. No—he was seducing her gently, and that was difficult to resist—but did she really want to?

Vanessa watched a downy woodpecker's arcing flight above the willows, as she matched her stride to the slow, rhythmic thrust of Shane's blades. So much about him was attractive to her—not just his physical presence, but his manner as well. She enjoyed his company, his charm and teasing ways, and admired what he was doing for Tommy. Unconsciously she tightened her fingers on his.

He turned to her and flashed a smile, the dimples playing in his cheeks. He's so handsome, she thought and returned his smile rather weakly before looking away. Was she falling in love?

Her feelings for him were real, she knew that. She also knew it would be very easy to become involved in the more intimate relationship he wanted—but where would it ultimately lead? He had made no pretense as to how he felt about marriage, and Vanessa knew that deeply held convictions didn't change easily. If they did become lovers, would he be capable of making the kind of commitment she needed? And without that commitment, what could possibly come out of the relationship for her but pain? She pushed a little harder on her skates, quickening the pace. She would have to tighten her resolve, and keep in control.

"I'M GOING TO MY ROOM," Vanessa said, after the early evening news the next day. "I've got a couple of book reviews to write up."

Cora looked up from the newspaper. "All right, dear. Could you tell Marcie that nature program she wanted to watch is starting in a few minutes?"

"Okay." Vanessa ran up the stairs and rapped her knuckles on the door to Marcie's room. "Gran says that show you wanted to watch is starting,'' she said, poking her head into the room.

Marcie put down her pen and rose from her desk, stretching. ''Okay. Thanks, Aunt Van.''

Vanessa smiled and continued down the hall to the narrow flight of stairs leading to her room. Once there, she turned on her stereo and, singing softly along to a song on the radio, lit a fire in the tiny parlor stove.

Sitting at her desk, she pulled two books from her briefcase and started reading. They were picture books, easy to skim through. She made note of the colorful illustrations and interesting text, writing a quick, favorable review for each.

Finished, she stood up and stretched, suddenly growing quite restless. She contemplated going for a walk, but could hear the wind through the eaves, blowing strong from the north, and was reluctant to leave her warm, cozy room.

She knelt on the floor in front of the fire, feeding it sticks of birch, enjoying the flashing sizzle of flame as it caught dry, papery bark. She switched off the radio and dropped in a cassette tape of her favorite Gershwin tunes. Smiling, she turned up the volume, enjoying the richness of the sound.

She moved the screen from in front of the whirlpool tub and turned on the taps, adding a splash of bubble bath. As the steamy fragrance began to rise, she stripped off her jeans and T-shirt. Slowly she slid into the hot, churning water, closing her eyes as a sigh of pleasure stirred delicate bubbles under her chin.

Head back and eyes closed, she smiled, remembering Shane's kiss. Her tongue flicked the corners of her mouth as she recalled the arousing touch of his lips, her instant response to their incredibly soft heat. She sighed again, dreamily this time.

Her smile changed suddenly to a frown and she sat up, abruptly stopping her thoughts from the direction they were taking. ''Enough already,'' she muttered to herself. Reaching for the sponge, she washed herself quickly, pulled the plug and stepped out. She took her robe from where it hung on the screen, put it on over her damp skin and tied the sash around her waist.

She didn't hear the knock on the door or see it open. She didn't see Shane standing in the doorway.

His eyes narrowed as he caught sight of her slim, robed figure. His nostrils flared as he caught the steamy scent of her bath water. Under cover of Gershwin, he stepped into the room, moving unhesitatingly across the floor to stand behind her.

Sensing something, Vanessa glanced over her shoulder, her eyes widening in shock. "Shane! What are you..." Her voice trailed off. Mesmerized by the desire she saw in his eyes, she stared back at him, knowing her eyes were still misted with her own desire.

"You have to be the sexiest woman I've ever seen," he said, his voice low and husky.

Vanessa took a step back, acutely conscious of the heat in his heavy-lidded eyes as he stared at her with wanting. She tightened the sash of her robe. "You shouldn't have come into my room like that," she said, tugging at the fine, silky material clinging to her damp skin.

"I know. But I'm glad I did." Shane turned and stared at her, his eyes still narrow with desire. He reached to pull the pins that held her hair, watching it fall, damp and curling, around her shoulders. "You're a beautiful, very desirable woman, Vanessa," he whispered huskily.

Her breath came a little faster and she swayed slightly, looking at him through half-closed eyes as her lips parted, inviting his kiss.

His eyes still on hers, he leaned forward until slowly, sensuously, his mouth came down on hers and she moaned softly against the flitting touch of his tongue against her lips, her cheeks, her neck. The sensation was exquisite, intensely arousing.

As he lifted his head, his eyes dropped from her flushed face and swollen lips, down the V of her robe to the swell of her breasts. Slowly he lowered his head, his mouth closing gently over a nipple thrust taut against the damp, silky material.

Vanessa's eyes closed on a sudden intake of breath and her hands came up to grasp the sides of his head, her fingers raking through his dark curls. She thrust her body against him, moaning loudly this time. This has to stop, she thought dazedly, trembling under his slow, sucking kisses. With great effort, she lowered her hands to his shoulders and pushed at him.

"Shane," she murmured. "Please, Shane—no more."

He straightened and stared down at her, a frown forming as he cupped her shoulders in his hands. "Why?" he whispered thickly.

Her lashes swept down and she shook her head, feeling confused. "I—I don't want to."

"Don't want to what, Vanessa?"

"Make love," she whispered.

"That's not what your body says," he muttered, pulling her close, again feeling her body meld instinctively to his.

With effort, she pushed away from him again. Hugging her arms tightly to herself, she managed to look at him. "Physically, I—I do want you," she whispered. It would be crazy to try to deny it. "But—I can't, Shane." She lifted her shoulders in a gesture of helplessness and struggled on, determined to be honest. "Not without love, and the trust and—and commitment that go along with it."

Shane ran a finger over the curve of her cheek and hooked it under her chin. "I'm damned tempted to change your mind."

"And I'm almost tempted to let you," Vanessa admitted. "But I wouldn't like either one of us very much afterward."

"Well, I guess then I won't be trying," Shane said, a dry smile twisting his lips as he moved his hand from her face and stepped away. "Tell me one thing, Vanessa," he said suddenly. "Have you ever made love to anyone but your ex-husband?"

Vanessa turned away from his speculative gaze. "No," she said shortly.

A smile eased over Shane's face and he nodded to himself. "Then, in a sense, the next time will be like the first, won't it?" He put his hands on her shoulders and turned her around to face him again. "I understand, Vanessa," he said softly, his eyes warm. "And I respect your decision. When I make love to you, it will be something we both want, with no reservations. The best things are worth waiting for. And Vanessa..." He kissed her softly on the lips. "We could have the best." Still smiling, he released her. "Maybe you should get dressed again," he said. "In case Marcie or Cora come up. We don't want them to get the wrong idea, do we?"

Vanessa shook her head, still feeling dazed and abstracted. While he wandered over to the stereo and began examining her collection of music, she picked up her clothes and stepped behind the screen, dressing quickly.

Is he sincere, she wondered suddenly, or a master of seduction? Did he honestly respect her feelings, or just realize that any pressure on his part would meet with greater resistance? She pushed her feet into well-worn slippers and tugged a comb through her hair, then stepped out from behind the screen. She looked at him crouched down by the stereo, firelight flickering over his strong, handsome face, and realized just how much she wanted to believe in his sincerity.

"So," she said lightly, "did Tommy's mother make it back today?"

Shane turned to smile at her. "Yes—we picked her up at the bus depot about four-thirty. She was a little taken aback by everything that had happened, but I took her to see Alma at the hospital and that seemed to put her mind at ease." He moved to sit against the cushions in front of the fire, patting the floor beside him. Vanessa added some wood and then sat down next to him.

"She's a very nice lady," he continued, his eyes on the eager flames. "I took her and Tommy out for a bite to eat before running them home, and we had time for a talk. She's almost fifty, you know, and finds it hard to keep up with Tommy at times. She's worried about all the potential for trouble that he's going to come across—it's not easy raising a young boy alone at her age. Anyway, I think she's ready to accept me as a friend and I'll probably continue to see Tommy outside of school." He grinned crookedly. "I grow more fond of the little guy all the time."

There was a sudden rap on the door and Marcie poked her head into the room. "Gran says come on down—she's made cocoa and snacks."

"Tell her we'll be right there," Vanessa said. She felt relieved. Shane might be playing it cool now, but she could still feel the lingering power of his kiss, the thrill of his touch. It would be so easy to turn to him, inviting his caresses.

"The voice of the chaperone," Shane said dryly. Suddenly he put an arm around her shoulders and pulled her to him. His mouth covered hers and he kissed her thoroughly, caressing the nape of her neck through strands of silky hair. With a stifled groan, he pushed away, regarding her flushed face and trembling lips through half-closed, smoldering eyes. "Vanessa, I—" He stopped and shook his head. Getting to his feet, he offered her a hand, pulling her up. For a moment she rested against him, feeling the taut power of his body against hers before he moved away.

"Let's get out of here while I still can," he said roughly.

"You go." Vanessa's voice was low. "I'll be there in a minute." She needed time to pull herself together.

With a brief nod, Shane left the room. Sighing, Vanessa shut the doors on the stove then went to splash cool water on her face.

Things were moving fast. Too fast. She had managed to apply the brakes that night, but would she have that much control next time? So much depended on Shane, and how long he would be willing to play it her way.

CHAPTER SIX

SNOW FELL SOFTLY, like a sigh in the darkness. It covered the streets and yards, clung to barren branches, hiding the drabness of late autumn and, for a time, it enchanted.

Vanessa knew it had snowed the moment she opened her eyes to the diffuse gray light. Getting out of bed, she slipped on her robe and knelt by the window looking down on the whiteness, enjoying its beauty. Then she grimaced as a car passed, leaving dark gray parallel tracks. She was thinking of the slippery drive to work that awaited her. For a moment she was tempted to crawl back into bed and curl up under the warm covers. Instead, she headed for the shower.

Shane had the right idea, she thought, working at home as he did. We should all be so lucky. She lifted her face to the hot, reviving spray, thinking of Shane with a smile.

She had seen a lot of him over the past couple of weeks, both in school and in her home. There had been little private time between them, and Vanessa was glad. It meant she didn't have to find the strength to resist him, to fight the passion he aroused in her.

She sighed and reached for the soap. She wanted him more and more with each passing day. Even without his kisses, she was aware of his desire for her. It was in his every look, in every casual touch of his hands. She wished she could succumb, give in to what her body demanded.

But she had emotional needs to consider. Could Shane meet them, satisfy her deep-seated need to be loved? Without love, what could they have together? They had friendship and could so easily have passion, but how long would it last?

Vanessa shut off the water and stepped out of the shower, reaching for a towel. She was beginning to have a strong feeling that a large part of Shane's attraction to her had to do with the fact that she hadn't succumbed to him. Perhaps she had become a challenge to him, a game of sorts. He knew he could storm her resolve with an onslaught of passion, but chose not to. Instead, he used a slow, subtle wooing of her senses, patiently waiting for her capitulation, waiting for her to come to him. He knew she eventually would, and Vanessa knew it, too.

She dried her hair and applied a bit of makeup. What would happen when she did stop fighting? She'd be foolish to think he'd want anything more than an affair. And when that affair was over... She shivered with a foreshadowing of pain.

"CHRISTMAS WILL BE HERE before we know it." Cora turned away from the kitchen window and its view of the freshly snow-covered yard.

"Just two and a half weeks now," Vanessa agreed. She glanced at the clock on the kitchen wall as she sipped her coffee.

"What are Shane's plans for Christmas?" Cora asked.

Vanessa shrugged. "I don't know, Gran. Why?"

"Well, I was thinking we should ask him here."

"I'm sure he has plans already." Vanessa took another swallow of coffee.

"Why don't you ask him and see? It can't hurt."

Vanessa looked at the clock again and stood up, finishing the last of her coffee on her way to the sink. "I've got to run," she said. "Traffic is going to be murder this morning with all that snow."

"Will you ask him?" Cora persisted.

"I'll ask him, but I'm sure he has other plans." She dropped a quick kiss on her grandmother's cheek. "Bye, Gran. See you tonight."

Traffic was every bit as bad as she'd expected. Drivers were slow and overcautious as they rediscovered winter-driving techniques, and as always, a car had stalled in the middle of a major intersection. By the time Vanessa got to school, she was feeling harried. Taking a few minutes to relax before starting the day, she stood by the library windows watching the children play.

Like all children, they found nothing but joy in the new snow. The sounds from the schoolyard were shrill and vibrant, carrying easily through to the library. Snowmen were being built and snowballs went flying whenever the yard supervisor's back was turned. Vanessa had to smile. Rules or no rules, who could resist a snowball fight?

The buzzer sounded on her phone. Turning away from the window, she picked up the receiver. "Library," she said.

"Good morning, library." Shane's voice was deep with amusement.

"Hello, Shane." She warmed instantly to the sound of his voice.

"Meet me for lunch today?" he asked.

"All right," Vanessa agreed readily. "Where?"

"Is Echo's all right?"

"That's fine." She glanced up as Bettina came into the room. "I've got to go now. See you there just after twelve?"

"I'll be there. See you then."

Vanessa replaced the receiver and smiled at Bettina. "Good morning."

"Good morning," Bettina said cheerfully, sitting on a corner of Vanessa's desk. "That, I take it, was lover boy?"

"It was Shane." Vanessa frowned. "Bettina—we're not—we're just friends," she insisted.

"Uh-huh." Bettina said, skeptically. "None of my friends look at me the way he looks at you, Van. I'd say you were very—friendly."

Vanessa scowled at her friend. "Bettina—"

Bettina held up her hands. "All right, all right. I won't tease. But—how are things between the two of you?"

Vanessa lifted her shoulders. "Like I said—friendly. At least, at the moment," she admitted ruefully. "He's a hard man to resist."

"I'll bet he is," Bettina said knowingly. "So—why do you?"

"Because maybe it'll hurt less when he goes on to someone else," Vanessa said quietly.

"Are you in love with him, Van?" Bettina asked softly.

Vanessa looked at her friend and smiled worriedly. "I'm afraid I am."

VANESSA STOOD by the entrance for a moment, letting her eyes adjust to the dim interior of the restaurant. She could see that Shane was already seated. He was holding the menu, one finger tapping against the edge as he stared absently into the candle flickering in the little lamp in front of him.

Vanessa watched him as she pulled off her gloves and unbuttoned her coat, admiring the strong line of his profile softened by the careless tumble of dark curls. Her heartbeat quickened as he looked up and saw her, his smile warm and welcoming.

She hung up her coat and approached the table slowly, still feeling a little bemused by what she had revealed to Bettina—and to herself. *I really do love him,* she thought dazedly, sitting across from him.

"Hi," she said, looking at him directly, her smile tentative.

"Hi." He smiled in return, eyeing her closely. "Vanessa—is something wrong?"

Everything, she thought with a stab of dismay. This wasn't supposed to happen to me. "No," she said. "I'm just hungry." She opened her menu and made a pretense of reading it. "What are you having?"

"A steak sandwich," he answered after another searching look at her face. "And you?"

"French onion soup. And a salad, I guess." As she closed the menu and laid it to one side, the waiter came to take their orders.

"Enjoying the snow?" Shane asked as the waiter left.

"Yes—and no. I enjoy the beauty of it when it's fresh like this, but I hate driving in it. And I love to watch the kids frolicking in the yard at school, especially the immigrant children. It's a real treat to see the looks on their faces when they see snow for the first time." She smiled. "They're delightful."

"Speaking of kids," Shane said, leaning back in his chair, "I've been wondering what to get Tommy for Christmas. I thought—" He broke off as the waiter placed their orders in front of them.

"You thought what?" Vanessa asked when they were alone again.

"Well, I'll have to talk to his mother first, but I thought he might like to have a dog."

"I think that's a great idea. Remember how he was with that puppy in the pet store?"

Shane nodded. "That's what gave me the idea. That, and—"

"And?" she prompted, stirring her soup with her spoon.

He shrugged. "It's just that I remember wanting a dog badly when I was about his age. That's all I wanted one Christmas." His eyes took on a distant look. "It's funny—I could see that dog so clearly, it was almost real to me. I was so sure I'd find it in a basket under the Christmas tree, complete with a big red bow around its neck."

"But you didn't get it," Vanessa stated quietly, reading the look of dismay on his face.

He smiled sardonically. "Oh, I got a dog, all right—a stuffed one." He shook his head. "It's funny how those childhood disappointments stay with us. I remember that Christmas clearer than any of the others." His lips tightened fractionally. "Holidays always seemed to bring out the worst in my parents. The fighting would escalate and—" He stopped abruptly and cut into his sandwich.

Remembering her own happy childhood and the magic she and her brother had felt each Christmas morning, Vanessa felt a stab of sympathy for the boy Shane had been. She pushed aside her half-finished soup and picked at her salad. "Will you take Tommy with you to pick out his puppy?" she asked.

"Definitely, providing his mother gives me the go-ahead. I think they're planning to go to Sterling over Christmas, so I'll wait until they get back."

"What are your plans for the holiday?"

He shrugged. "I've got a couple of possibilities, but nothing definite yet."

Vanessa poked at her salad. "Gran wants me to ask you to come over to our place." She tried to sound casual.

"I'd like that," he responded instantly. "Providing the invitation comes from you as well as your grandmother."

She looked up. "Of course it does," she said with sincerity. "We'd all love to have you. Ben and Bettina will be there as well, along with their daughter, Haili."

Shane reached across the table and took her hand in his, squeezing her fingers gently. "Count me in, too," he said, his eyes smiling into hers. "I'd love to spend Christmas with you, Vanessa."

THE DAYS leading up to Christmas flew by in a flurry of shopping. Vanessa found it easy to buy presents for Marcie and Cora. Cora was always happy with books, while Marcie loved new clothes. Finding a gift for Shane presented more of a problem. After much thought and searching, she found something she thought was perfect and only hoped that he'd think so, too.

"Let's save decorating the tree until Christmas Eve this year," Cora suggested.

Vanessa's eyebrows arched in surprise. "Why so late, Gran?"

"I thought Shane would probably enjoy helping with it," Cora said, knitting needles clicking as she talked.

"But he isn't coming over until—" Vanessa stopped, her eyes narrowing. "Gran—what have you been up to?"

"Nothing, dear. I just suggested to Shane that he come over Christmas Eve and spend the night." She looked up from her knitting, her smile complacent. "He seemed quite happy to accept. You don't mind, do you?"

"Gran." Vanessa feigned annoyance. "What a sneaky trick. And I love you for it."

CHRISTMAS EVE ARRIVED along with the first real cold spell of the season. Vanessa opened the door to Shane, who came in with a rush of cold air, his arms laden with gaily wrapped packages.

"Santa Claus, I presume," she said, taking the packages from him.

"This is one Santa Claus who's glad to forgo a trip around the world in favor of sitting in front of a warm fire tonight," he said, rubbing his hands together. "It's cold out there!" Unzipping his parka, he pulled out a shoe box with holes punched in the sides. "This," he said, "is Frankie."

Vanessa looked at the box warily. "Frankie?" she asked.

Shane grinned. "Nothing scaly. It's a canary for Cora. Do you think she'll like it?"

"She'll love it," Vanessa stated, delighted.

"Good. I've got the cage in the car. Hold him while I run out and get it." He handed her the box and dashed outside.

Putting the box down on the hall table, Vanessa poked her head into the living room. "We'll be in in a few minutes," she told Cora and Marcie. "Shane's getting something from his car and then I'm going to show him to his room."

"Don't be long," Marcie implored. "I can't stand looking at this bare tree any longer. It feels so unChristmassy."

"Hang in there, kid. It won't be long now." She went back into the hall as the door opened and Shane came in, bird cage dangling from his fingers.

Putting the cage down, he shrugged off his parka, hanging it in the closet. He turned to Vanessa, his eyes warm in his cold-reddened cheeks. "Hi," he said softly.

"Hi," she returned, her lashes sweeping down. She felt his hands on her shoulders and looked up to meet his eyes. He dropped a quick kiss on her lips.

"I don't suppose we get to share a room tonight," he murmured.

"And shock my dear old grandmother?" Vanessa said lightly, although she had a sneaking suspicion that Cora would be more approving than shocked. "No, Shane. Your room is between Gran's and Marcie's. Here—let me get Frankie and I'll show you." She ducked from his grasp and picked up the bird.

"Right between the chaperones." He sighed dejectedly. "There'll be no sneaking up the back stairs tonight!"

"Shane," Vanessa began sternly.

"I know, I know. Behave myself." He shook his head as he picked up his overnight case and followed her up the stairs. "At times, Ms Evans," he said, "you are very much the schoolteacher."

It was funny, Vanessa reflected as she showed Shane to his room, how his teasing references to their sleeping together didn't bother her. Not to take him seriously was easy, as she admonished him in what he called her schoolmarm voice. No, she thought, watching him lay his suitcase on the foot of the bed, his teasing didn't bother her at all. It was those sudden looks through heavy-lidded eyes, looks that said without doubt that he wanted her, that were troubling.

"Is Frankie going to be all right in that box?" she asked, putting it down on the dresser, hearing the scrabble of tiny feet inside.

"He'll be fine. I'll put him in the cage later tonight—it's too cold for him right now."

"Are you ready then?"

"Ready—lead me to that fire."

"We've got lots to do tonight," she told him, flicking out the light as they left the room. "Gran thought you'd like to help with the tree so we left the decorating until tonight."

"Sounds like fun," Shane said agreeably, following her down the stairs. "I haven't decorated a tree in years."

"Don't you have one in your apartment?"

Shane shook his head. "There doesn't seem to be much point. I'm not usually home much over Christmas."

"How do you usually spend the holidays?" Vanessa asked curiously.

Shane shrugged. "There's usually a party going on somewhere."

The idea of spending Christmas going from one impersonal party to another sounded cold and lonely to Vanessa. Christmas without a family and the accumulation of traditions must be a sad time. Like the first Christmas after the accident, she reflected, her eyes darkening briefly. Even now the holidays didn't pass without some recollection of Christmas days long past when her parents and brother were part of her life. They were happy memories, but always tinged with a sadness that came from knowing that memories were all that was left of that loving closeness.

Cora and Marcie were waiting for them in the living room. There was a fire burning brightly opposite the corner where a tall, spreading evergreen waited to be dressed. Marcie knelt by a box of ornaments, carefully unwrapping the star that was to shine from the top of the deep green branches.

"Hi, Shane," Marcie said, turning as he came in, her eyes bright with excitement. "You came just in time. I got the lights all straightened out, Aunt Van," she continued. "Can we start now?"

"Go ahead." Vanessa smiled, glad to see childlike excitement still alive in her niece. She was growing up so fast.

"Hello, Shane," Cora said with a fond smile. "Is it getting cold out?"

"Frigid is more like it, Cora," Shane said. He stood with his back to the fire, hands in the pockets of his gray flannel slacks. "It's a good feeling to be inside on a night like this. I want to thank you for having me."

Cora waved a hand dismissingly. "We're happy to have you here with us." Her eyes twinkled suddenly. "I must admit, it's nice to have a man around."

Shane's dimples flashed in a wide smile. "What man wouldn't want to be with three such lovely ladies?"

Always the charmer, Vanessa thought with a little smile. "Would you like something to drink, Shane? Eggnog, maybe? We keep the rum to a minimum."

"That sounds good. Thanks, Vanessa."

"Gran?"

"Yes, please, dear."

"Me, too?" asked Marcie.

"A small one," Vanessa consented, ladling eggnog from the punch bowl on the side table near the archway to the dining room. She handed out the small crystal glasses filled with the creamy drink. "Now let's get that tree decorated," she said.

The decorations were like a box full of memories, a hodgepodge of ornaments gathered over the years and kept carefully, brought out from one Christmas to the next. Vanessa touched the glittering star, remembering the year her father had brought it home and how he had lifted her high into the air so she could put it on top of the tree. Then there were her mother's favorite ceramic snowflakes, and the roughly carved and painted reindeer David had made when he was younger than his daughter was now.

What were Shane's memories of Christmas? Vanessa wondered, watching him join in easily. He was assigned the task of placing the ornaments on the highest branches. He had said the fighting between his parents had usually worsened over the holidays. What could it have been like growing up in that kind of atmosphere? The tension must have been unbearable at times. The scars must be deep, she thought. Would they ever heal completely?

"It looks great," Marcie said when all the ornaments had found their place on the tree. "Let's get the presents under it."

"Mine are in my bedroom closet, Marcie," Cora said. "Could you bring them down for me please, dear?"

"Sure, Gran. How about you, Aunt Van? Should I get yours, too?"

"Please. They're on my bed. No snooping, kiddo," she called as Marcie dashed out of the room.

Marcie returned and carefully placed the armloads of gifts under the tree, while Vanessa hung up the Christmas stockings.

"Ah, good," Cora approved. "I see you got one for Shane, too."

Shane's eyebrows rose. "A stocking?"

"I'm sure Santa will want to fill it." Vanessa grinned at him, tacking the red-and-green-striped stocking to the mantel.

"That's all the gifts," Marcie said, sitting back on her heels and admiring the colorful stack under the tree with satisfaction. "I can hardly wait."

"Just a few more hours, Marcie." Vanessa smiled. "And then you can rip into them."

"Yeah." Marcie's eyes gleamed with anticipation. "Can we play some games now?"

"Let's put on some music first," Cora suggested. "*The Nutcracker Suite*, Vanessa?"

"That old stuff," Marcie groaned as Vanessa dropped the cassette into the tape deck.

"Good music is ageless," Cora said to Marcie. "And Tchaikovsky is much more appropriate on Christmas Eve than—than . . ." She looked at Vanessa for help.

"Bryan Adams? Glass Tiger? Madonna?" Vanessa laughed, naming some of Marcie's favorites.

"Those are the ones." Cora nodded. "Now—get that Monopoly board set up, Marcie. I feel lucky tonight."

The evening passed pleasantly. Shane's presence was a welcome addition to Christmas Eve and he seemed to enjoy their company as much as they enjoyed his. After cocoa and snacks, Cora and Marcie said their good-nights.

"Are you staying up?" Shane asked Vanessa.

She nodded. "I'm not sleepy yet—Gran and Marcie are the early birds around here. Besides, I've got to play Santa. It's my job to fill the stockings," she explained. "And when Marcie was little, I used to sneak her gifts down after she was asleep." She sighed reflectively. "She's growing up so fast, Shane. She's not a little girl anymore." She pushed her feelings of nostalgia aside and turned to Shane. "Would you like some brandy?"

"A small one, please." He threw a birch log onto the fire and watched the flames lick eagerly at the bark while Vanessa poured their drinks.

"Thanks," he said absently, accepting a glass from her and taking a sip.

Vanessa stood quietly at his side, staring into the fire. It felt so good, so right to have him there that night. It's as if he belongs with us, she thought, a wistful smile curving her lips. She stole a glance at his strong profile, feeling a sudden rush of love for him. Wanting badly to touch him, she put a hand on his arm and squeezed her fingers briefly.

Instantly her hand was covered by his, holding it against corded muscles. "I want to thank you," he said, his voice low, "for asking me into your home tonight. It's been a great evening."

"I'm glad you're here," she whispered, her eyes sliding away from his lest he see just how glad she was. This man made her feel so very vulnerable.

He ran a finger lightly from the hand that still rested on his arm, over her shoulder and up to hook under her chin, forcing her to look at him. His eyes smiled into hers as he lowered his head to kiss her.

Vanessa murmured her pleasure against warm, brandied lips, savoring every nuance of his kiss.

It was far too brief. Shane stepped back suddenly, but it was only to pluck the glass from her fingers and place it with his on the mantel. Eyes searing into hers, he pulled her into his arms, his mouth hot and demanding as his hands cupped her hips and thrust them tight against the intoxicating tautness of his.

For a moment it was all she wanted, to be lost to the need surging through her, but deep inside, the tiny voice of reason persisted in being heard. She knew she shouldn't let herself be carried away any further. She shouldn't. Her hands knotted into fists, resisting the urge to splay over his back and pull him closer. This has to stop, she thought through a daze of desire. It has to.

Sensing her withdrawal, Shane pulled back with a difficulty she could see, looking at her through dark, hooded eyes.

Her own eyes mirrored her confusion and she returned his look unsteadily. Weakening to the ache of arousal throbbing between her legs, she swayed toward him, her lips parted and inviting, hungering for his.

"Vanessa." The warning note in his voice stopped her. "I'm fighting very hard right now to keep from making love to you. If I kiss you again . . ." He stopped, looking closely at her. "What is it you want, Vanessa?" he asked huskily.

She hesitated, catching her bottom lip nervously between her teeth, aching for him, afraid to submit to her desire.

Shane sighed heavily in frustration. "I want to make love to you badly. But I'm not so sure it's what you want. And until it is—" He moved away from her and picked up his brandy glass, staring moodily into the fire.

"Shane, I—" Vanessa stopped and shrugged helplessly. She lifted her glass with an unsteady hand and took a drink. How could she tell him of the fears that held her back from his embrace? She wanted him, but she also loved him. She couldn't make love with him and not worry about the pain that was sure to follow. He had made it all too clear that he wasn't a man for commitments. No matter how much he might desire her, he didn't love her. And when that desire had been sated, he would move on, leaving her with more heartache than she could bear.

She took another sip of brandy. "Shane, I do want you." Her voice was low as she stared into the fire. "But that's not a part of me I can give lightly." She risked a quick look at him. "I want to thank you for respecting that and for not—not trying to persuade me." Her lips flickered with a wry smile. Did he have any idea how easy that would be?

"I'm not a saint, Vanessa," he said, frowning deeply. "Stopping myself from making love to you was—is damned hard. I'm not always going to be able to step back like I just did."

"Maybe I won't always want you to," she admitted, her lashes sweeping down to cover her eyes.

"Vanessa—" Shane let out a deep, ragged breath and dragged his fingers through his hair. "Drop it," he demanded roughly, "or you're going to find out just how far from sainthood I really am." He took a swallow of brandy. "Didn't you have to play Santa Claus or something?"

"Right." Vanessa put her glass down. "I'll go get the presents," she said, glad for the excuse to leave the room. She needed a few minutes away from him to restore her equilibrium. Going to the hall closet, she took out a shopping bag overflowing with small, brightly wrapped gifts. She came back into the living room and put the bag down on the hearth.

"Can I help?" Shane swallowed the last of his brandy and put the glass down.

Vanessa glanced at him. His eyes were clear gray again and he managed a pleasant, if somewhat forced, smile. The crisis had passed. "Okay," she said, feeling relieved. "Each present should have a name tag. Marcie has the polka-dot stocking, Gran's is red and mine is green. You've got the stripes."

"You didn't have to bother about one for me," Shane said, delving into the shopping bag.

"Sure we did," Vanessa said, feeling more cheerful with every passing minute. "It wouldn't have been much fun for us to open ours while you sat there with nothing, would it?"

As they filled the stockings, the tension remaining between them dispersed and Vanessa breathed a sigh of relief. She enjoyed the friendly, teasing side of their relationship so much. Crumpling the empty shopping bag, she threw it into the fire. "I'm off to bed," she said lightly. "Feel free to stay up, if you want."

"I think I will," Shane said. He stood with his back to the fire, hands in the pockets of his slacks.

"Can I get you anything?"

He shook his head. "Nothing, thanks. Good night, Vanessa."

"Good night, Shane." She risked giving him a quick kiss. "See you in the morning." She left him staring broodingly at the lights flickering on the Christmas tree.

"VANESSA."

Vanessa gave a mew of protest and burrowed deeper under the covers, trying to recapture the gossamer threads of her dream. A hand closed over her shoulder and shook gently.

"It's Christmas morning, lazybones. Don't you want to see what Santa brought?"

Vanessa opened one eye and stared blurrily at Shane sitting on the padded edge of her bed. "Go away," she muttered.

"Uh-uh. We drew straws to see who would wake you up," he said, his eyes laughing. "I lost."

Moaning sleepily, Vanessa rubbed her eyes. "What time is it?"

"Eight-thirty. We can't wait any longer to open our presents even if you can. We're giving you fifteen minutes." He put a hand on the mattress and pressed firmly, causing the water to roll under her. "C'mon, lazy lady," he drawled. "Up and at 'em. Coffee's on, and I've whipped up a batch of melt-in-your-mouth pancakes." He pushed on the mattress again.

"Okay, okay." Vanessa scowled at him. "I'm up."

"You're still prone. I'm not leaving until your head is off that pillow."

Vanessa pushed herself up, letting her head loll against the headboard. "There," she muttered, running her fingers through tousled hair. "I'm up."

"I can't believe that anyone who looks so soft and cuddly while sleeping can be so prickly. Like a porcupine." He chuckled. "Maybe I should nickname you Porky."

She glared at him. "You do and I'll belt you one."

Shane laughed, his eyes gleaming. "I thought your hit list only included liars, bullies and cheats."

"I forgot to add unbearably cheerful morning people." She yawned and stretched. "I'm up for sure," she said. "Go away and let me get dressed."

"Can I stay and watch? I want to see what's under that heavy-duty nightgown."

"Shane—get lost."

"Okay, I'm going. But first—" He leaned forward and kissed her. "Merry Christmas, lovely lady," he murmured against her lips. He kissed her again, quickly this time, as if he dared not linger. "You've got ten minutes left," he said, glancing at his watch as he stood up.

Vanessa watched him leave the room, a smile playing on her lips. I love him so much, she thought. If only— She frowned and pushed the thought aside. She wasn't going to let doubts about the future ruin today. She was going to make the best of the time she had with Shane, gather a storehouse of memories to sustain her when he was no longer part of her life.

After a quick wash, she pulled on black slacks and a bulky sweater and ran downstairs to join the others in the kitchen.

"Merry Christmas, Aunt Van!" Marcie, cheeks flushed with excitement got up from the table and gave her a big hug.

"Merry Christmas, sweetie." Vanessa returned the hug and gave her an affectionate kiss. "Did you save some pancakes for me?"

"Lots. I'll get 'em." Marcie took a plate from the table and went to the oven.

"Merry Christmas, Gran." Vanessa stooped to kiss Cora's cheek.

"Merry Christmas, dear." Cora smiled fondly at her granddaughter. "Did you sleep well?"

"Until I was rudely awakened—right in the middle of a great dream, too." She made a face at Shane, who was sitting across the table from Cora.

"Aren't you going to wish me a merry Christmas, too?" he asked plaintively.

"Merry Christmas, Shane."

"What—don't I get a kiss?"

"You already—" Flustered, Vanessa stopped and glanced quickly at Cora.

"Just a little one," he coaxed, inclining his head and tapping his cheek with a lean forefinger. "That's all I ask."

"Go on, Vanessa." Cora laughed. "Give the poor man a kiss."

Vanessa went around the table and bent to kiss Shane's cheek. He turned his head as her lips touched his cheek, capturing them with his, and kissed her with a thoroughness that left her flushed and breathless.

"Merry Christmas, Vanessa," he said, a soft, teasing gleam in his eyes.

Vanessa looked at Cora, who was smiling with obvious satisfaction. Marcie set a plate of pancakes down on the table, grinning widely.

"He makes great pancakes, too, Aunt Van," she said, her eyes sparkling with laughter.

Vanessa sat down rather abruptly, feeling as if they were ganging up on her. Cora and Marcie, she knew, were excited because they thought wedding bells weren't far off. She would have to tell them that was the last thing they should expect. Whatever her relationship with Shane was, whatever it might become, he had made it clear that marriage did not enter into his plans for the future.

"Better hurry, Vanessa," Cora said, breaking into her reverie. "I don't think we can restrain Marcie much longer."

"All those presents just sitting under that tree waiting to be ripped open," Marcie said with a groan. "I can hardly stand it."

"Then let's get at them." Vanessa struggled with one last mouthful of pancake and then pushed her plate away with an apologetic look at Shane. "It's too early to swallow anything but coffee," she said. "I'll try again later."

"Cold pancakes?" he said, his eyebrows rising.

"With peanut butter." She grinned, getting up from the table to add more coffee to her cup. "Let's leave everything in here as is and start on those presents."

"All right!" Marcie was up from the table and through the door to the living room in a flash. Laughing at her eagerness, the others followed.

A fire had been lit earlier and Shane added another log to the crackling blaze. Sunshine streamed warmly through the southern window, shining on the ornaments dangling gently from the tree. They delved into the stockings first, exclaiming over the abundance of small gifts, most of which were either practical or humorous.

"I'm going upstairs for the bird," Shane said in an aside to Vanessa. "Be right back."

As Marcie sorted through the mound of gifts under the tree, Shane came back into the room.

"This is for you, Cora," he said, placing the loosely wrapped bird cage at her feet. He had moved it into the cage before going to sleep the night before. "I hope you like it."

Eyes widening with pleasure, Cora slipped off the blue bow holding the silver paper in place. A tiny yellow canary hopped onto one of the perches and regarded her with bright black eyes. "Oh, Shane!" Cora exclaimed with delight. "He's lovely. Thank you!"

"You're welcome, Cora." Shane looked pleased. "His name is Frankie—he's three months old and guaranteed to sing for you."

Cora smiled happily. "Frankie. I like that." She looked up at Shane with a fond smile. "Thank you again. It's a lovely gift."

It was, Vanessa thought. And thoughtful, too. Cora would especially enjoy the bird during the day when no one else was home.

"Shane's turn," Marcie said, handing him a small package. "It's from me."

"Thank you, Marcie." Shane smiled with open affection at the girl as he sat on the couch and opened the present. It was a bottle of after-shave.

"I tried all kinds," Marcie volunteered and added with a grin, "and I made sure Aunt Vanessa liked it before I bought it."

Shane chuckled. "Good thinking, kid." He removed the top and sniffed. "And you've got good taste. Thanks."

"Give him my present next, Marcie," Cora insisted. "It's that blue-and-red one in the corner—that one." She pointed to it.

Cora had knitted him a thick wool sweater in a deep royal blue. "I sneaked the measurements from your jacket one evening," she explained. "It should fit."

Shane was obviously pleased as he examined the sweater. "Thank you, Cora," he said, kissing her warmly on the cheek.

Marcie opened her gift from Shane next. He had given her a small plush unicorn. Around its neck was a delicate gold chain. Marcie unfastened it and held it up delightedly. "Thanks, Shane," she said, her face flushed with pleasure.

"It's—they're beautiful." Smiling happily, she let Vanessa fasten the chain around her neck.

Another thoughtful gift, Vanessa mused, struggling with the tiny clasp. He had unerringly appealed to both the child and the woman in Marcie.

After another pleased smile at Shane, Marcie knelt in front of the tree again. "Ah—here's one for you, Aunt Van. From Shane," she added. Her eyes curious, she sat back on her heels to watch Vanessa open it.

Vanessa turned the flat, foil-wrapped package over in her hand, running a finger under the tape at one end.

Marcie groaned impatiently. "C'mon, Aunt Van! Rip into it!"

Laughing, Vanessa did just that. Inside the box was a brass-rimmed crystal butterfly just larger than the palm of her hand. Exclaiming softly with pleasure, she held it up to catch the light. A spatter of rainbows whirled around the room.

"Oh, Shane—it's stunning. Thank you!" She smiled warmly at him.

He smiled in return. "You're welcome, Vanessa."

"Is his name Bertie?" she asked teasingly.

"It did cross my mind," he admitted, chuckling. "But— did you know Vanessa means butterfly?" His eyes held hers.

"Does it?" Vanessa looked away from him. Oh, Shane, she thought with dismay, why do you have to be so utterly irresistible? "I'll hang it in my room, in the south gable," she said, keeping her voice light. "It gets lots of sunlight."

"This is yours from Aunt Van." Marcie handed Shane a large, cream-colored envelope sashed with a bright red ribbon.

Vanessa held her breath while he opened it. Would he approve?

The envelope contained an eight-by-ten photograph of a puppy. Shane pulled it out and looked at it, then at her, puzzled.

"That's Sasha," Vanessa explained a little nervously. "An Alaskan Malamute cross—she's two months old. I arranged with the owners to keep her until you move out of the city. But if you would rather not have a dog, well, I can cancel—"

"Don't you dare!" A pleased expression was spreading across Shane's face. "I had every intention of getting a dog as soon as I could—and this one is perfect. Thank you, Vanessa. Thank you very much."

"Isn't she cute?" Marcie put in eagerly. "I went with Aunt Van to help pick her out. She's just a big, cuddly ball of fur. You'll love her, Shane. And the breeder said you can go visit the dog any time, keep her on weekends and that. They don't live that far from your house," she added. "Only ten miles or so. We drew a map on the back of the picture."

Shane glanced at it briefly and nodded. "Good. I'll have to get out there soon." He smiled at Vanessa.

Vanessa returned his smile with relief. She hadn't been all that sure that he really wanted a dog, but he'd left her with no doubt that he was pleased with the gift.

"My turn again!" Marcie dived under the tree to retrieve a large box. She held it up and shook it experimentally. "Are these those boots I wanted, Gran?"

After the rest of the gifts had been opened and the colorful debris cleared away, Vanessa glanced at the clock on the mantel. "The Blakelys will be here soon," she said. "It's time to get the bird in the oven. We eat Christmas dinner about three," she explained to Shane as she stood to go to the kitchen.

"Let me lend a hand," Shane said. He got up and stretched lithely.

Vanessa pushed through the kitchen door. "There isn't all that much to do just now. We got everything ready yesterday. The turkey is ready for the oven and all the vegetables are ready to cook." She slid the roaster in the oven. "There." She shut the oven door and turned around. "Now,

I think I could eat one of those pancakes of yours before I go shower and change."

Shane put his hands on her shoulders. "Vanessa."

"Mm?" For a moment she leaned against him, feeling his breath stir her hair.

"Thank you again," he said. "For Sasha. And for a most memorable Christmas morning." He kissed her softly, savoring her lips, his hands tightening as she sighed and melded against him.

Reluctantly Vanessa pulled away after a moment, not wanting the kiss to deepen into the passion they had experienced the night before. "I'm hungry," she said.

"So am I," Shane murmured, pulling her back into his arms, kissing her hard with a passion she'd never known.

Her own hunger for him welled and for an uncontrollable moment, she pressed hard against him, returning his kiss urgently. Then, with difficulty, she pushed away, holding her arms tight against her chest as she struggled to subdue her wanting.

"Now I'm starving," Shane said huskily, his eyes hooded and dark.

"Shane, I—" She bit her bottom lip and turned away. This was getting crazy.

"I know," he sighed, touching her shoulders lightly. "Listen—you go have that shower now. I'll clean up."

Vanessa nodded abruptly and with a rather tight smile, left the room, all thoughts of eating gone. Food would not satisfy the kind of hunger inside her.

"I'm going to shower and change," she said to Cora and Marcie. "Marcie—Shane's in the kitchen clearing up the breakfast dishes. Could you please give him a hand?"

Marcie began to clap lazily, a grin splitting her face.

Vanessa paused in the doorway, sighed and shook her head. "No, Marcie. I mean, go help the man."

Marcie got to her feet. "Yes, ma'am. Do you want me to set the dining-room table yet?"

"You can wait for Haili if you want. You know she likes to help."

"Yeah, okay." Marcie pushed through the kitchen door. "Hey, Shane—Aunt Van says I'm supposed to give you a hand."

Vanessa heard the sound of applause again and shared a smile of fond exasperation with Cora before going upstairs.

She had hoped the hot, hard spray of water would distract her from thinking about Shane and the kisses they had shared. If anything, the memories became more vivid as the water pelted her body, and she moaned with dismay. She knew her ability to fight her feelings diminished with every kiss, with his every touch. She longed to be able to ignore nagging reason, to release her love and accept whatever Shane could offer. The problem was that, without his love, it would never be enough.

After the shower, she dried her hair into soft golden-brown waves that swirled and shimmered against her shoulders. She applied makeup expertly, a dark eyeliner emphasizing her green-gold eyes. Her dress was a deep-green sheath with belted waist, long cuffed sleeves and a low-cut neckline. After adding a thick gold chain and diamond stud earrings, she dabbed on perfume and then stepped back to examine herself in the mirror. She fluffed her hair a bit and then turned to go downstairs. Shane would approve, she knew, already imagining the glint of admiration in his eyes.

Attracting him wasn't the problem, she thought as she made her way downstairs. He was already interested, as much as any man had been. If only she could be satisfied with that.

"Wow! Hey—you look great, Aunt Vanessa," Marcie approved enthusiastically as Vanessa came into the living room.

"Very pretty," agreed Cora.

Shane turned from the fire to look at her, his eyes lingering on every silk-covered curve. "Stunning," he said finally, his voice low and intimate, as though they were alone in the room. "You are very beautiful, Vanessa."

"Thank you," she murmured, her face flushed with pleasure. "I—I think I'll go check on the turkey."

"In that dress?" Cora shook her head as she got up from her chair. "I'll see to it."

"I was going to put on an apron, Gran."

"You just sit and take it easy for a while. You'll be busy enough later on. Maybe I'm not a great cook, but I can baste a bird as well as the next person. Besides, I think I'll make a pot of tea."

With no excuse to leave the room, Vanessa sat on a chair near the fire, nervously aware that Shane was still watching her, his eyes hooded and desiring.

"I think I'll go up to my room and try on some of these new clothes," Marcie said, gathering up an armful of presents. "I sure hope that purple shirt fits," she added, heading into the hallway. "I'd really like to wear it today. It'll go great with those black stretch pants."

Shane waited until Marcie left the room and they could hear her footsteps on the stairs. "Vanessa, come here," he demanded softly.

She looked at him as he stood, back to the fire. His hands were in the pockets of his slacks, straining the material across his hips. Dark curls tumbled above intense, light gray eyes. "What for?" she asked, getting up slowly, knowing full well what he wanted and wanting it, too.

"I have this irresistible urge to kiss you," he said huskily. Taking her hands in his, he pulled her to him. "Indulge me," he whispered, his eyes burning into hers. "It's Christmas."

With a quiet moan, Vanessa raised her lips to meet his, releasing her desire for him. His lips welded to hers with a passion that made her quiver weakly. Freeing his hand from hers, he cupped the silken curve of her hips and pulled her tight against him. "Ah, Vanessa," he groaned against her mouth. "You're driving me wild. I want you so damned bad."

He kissed her again, his hips thrusting forcefully against hers. Then, with an abruptness that left her dazed and trembling, he pushed her away from him.

"Enough of that," he said thickly, "or your grandmother is going to be in for one hell of a shock when she comes through that door."

Vanessa caught her bottom lip between her teeth and turned away from him. Holding her arms tight against her chest, she stared into the fire, fighting the pain of thwarted desire. "Shane, I—I'm not..." She drew a deep breath and started again, her voice low and unsteady. "I don't want you to think that I'm leading you on—teasing you. I'm not going to try and pretend I don't want you, but—"

"You're not ready," he finished flatly. Sighing heavily with frustration, he raked his fingers through his hair.

I'm more than ready, she thought wryly, wishing she could tell him her fears. *I'm scared because I love you,* she wanted to say, *scared because you'll hurt me whether you mean to or not.* "I'd explain if I could," she said diffidently.

He reached out to run a hand caressingly over her arm. "You're worth waiting for," he said roughly. "And when we do make love—" His kiss was brief but explosive with the promise of passion to come.

When we do make love, Vanessa thought as he moved away from her again. It was as inevitable as night following day, she knew, unless she stopped seeing him. She glanced at him out of the corner of her eye, knowing there was no way on earth she was going to do that. He meant too much to her already. Bettina, Ben and Haili arrived, their arms laden with gifts. Vanessa felt her mood lighten in the face of their high spirits and laughter.

"Whew!" Ben said, closing the door behind him. "It's cold enough out there to set those proverbial brass monkeys singing soprano!" He shrugged off his coat and handed it to Vanessa. "Whoa!" he ordered as she started to move away. He pulled a plastic piece of mistletoe from his shirt pocket and held it above his shaggy blond head. "Pucker up, Van." He grinned. "I've been waiting for this."

Laughing, Vanessa kissed him. "Ben, you're incorrigible. How do you put up with him, Bettina?"

Bettina sighed in resignation. "It isn't easy. But—while we're at it—Merry Christmas, Shane." She took his hand in hers and kissed him warmly on each cheek.

"Merry Christmas, Bettina—Ben." Shane smiled.

Ben clasped Shane's hand, shaking it heartily. "Good to see you, Shane," he said in his deep, booming voice. "It's great to have another man around. Maybe I can get out of kitchen detail now."

"No way, Ben," Vanessa vetoed. "Shane is every bit as liberated as you pretend to be. He's already volunteered to help with the cooking." She laughed at Ben's growl of protest.

"I brought dessert," Bettina said, handing Cora a covered plate. "It's a chocolate mousse with almonds and Amaretto." She removed her coat to reveal a clinging burgundy jumpsuit with a silver chain belted around her waist.

"It tastes great," Haili volunteered. "I got to lick the bowl. Hey, Marcie—I got that stereo I wanted after all, and a bunch of tapes. What'd you get?"

"Lots of clothes," Marcie answered. "And those boots I wanted. Hey, and Gran got a canary from Shane. Want to go see him? He's in the kitchen."

"Yeah, sure. Then we can go open the presents. Wait till you see what I got for you." The two girls chatted their way to the kitchen.

"We've had our ears blasted all morning," Bettina groaned. "Whose idea was that stereo, anyway?" She looked accusingly at Ben. "I never thought I'd long for the days when all we heard was Raffi's 'Baby Beluga' played nonstop!"

The adults settled in the living room. As Vanessa poured sherry for Bettina and Cora and Scotch for Ben, Shane stoked up the fire until it crackled brightly.

"Thanks, Van." Ben accepted his drink from her and took a swallow. "Ah. That's perfect." He settled back comfortably in his chair, stretching his long legs out in front of him. "We've been up since six," he said. "Haili couldn't hold out any longer than that."

"Enjoy it while you can," Cora advised. "It won't last much longer. I miss having a young child around at Christmas. Marcie's still got a bit of the little girl in her, but it's disappearing fast." She sighed. "She'll be sixteen in March."

"You need to get after that granddaughter of yours to supply you with some more great-grandchildren," Ben drawled with an audacious wink at Vanessa. "It's about time she started reproducing."

To Vanessa's relief, Bettina caught Ben's eye and gave her head a slight warning shake. She knew the subject was a little too close to home for Vanessa to take lightly, as she usually did when Ben teased.

At that moment Marcie and Haili came into the room, canned soft drinks in hand. "That's a neat bird, Mrs. Evans," Haili said with her girlish grin. "Frankie—I like that name." She flopped down on the floor by the tree, crossing her long, thin legs under her. "Can we open our presents to each other now?"

"Haven't you had enough presents yet?" her father asked.

"Uh-uh. No way. Never!" She sighed happily, sorting through the remaining packages. "I just love exchanging presents—and I love Christmas."

Everyone helped with the final dinner preparations. Marcie and Haili set the dining-room table with great care, using Cora's best china on a rose-colored damask cloth. Crystal and silver sparkled under the chandelier and the candles nestled in tiny wreaths of holly.

There was a warm, friendly atmosphere around the table, gay with laughter and gentle teasing. Christmas music played softly in the background.

"I'd like to make a toast," Cora said, holding up a crystal wine glass. "To friends, old and new." She smiled at Shane. "Merry Christmas, everyone."

"Merry Christmas." The words echoed around the table to the clink of glasses.

"I LIKE YOUR SHANE A LOT," Bettina said to Vanessa later as they finished clearing up the kitchen. "My advice is—keep him."

"He's not mine to keep," Vanessa protested, wiping the sink. "I would, but—" She sighed. "I don't know, Bettina. I can't help but feel as though every minute with him is—well, borrowed time." She put down the cloth and leaned against the countertop, arms crossed. "He's not going to stay around, Bettina," she said, her voice low and troubled. "I—I can sense it. I'm a challenge to him, as much as anything. Once we make love—" She stopped and smiled ruefully. "It's inevitable. I'm fighting a battle I really don't want to fight. And once he's—he's satisfied, he'll move on, I know he will." She tightened her arms against her chest, a line of pain cutting her brow. "It's going to hurt so bad," she whispered.

"Come on, girl! Where's your confidence?" Bettina shook her head. "He doesn't give me the impression that he's hanging around just waiting for the opportunity to jump on your bones. He likes you, Van!"

"Like isn't enough, Bettina." Vanessa smiled sadly. "Not with this man. I want his love...and I'm not sure he can give it, not to one woman. He had an unhappy childhood—parents who fought constantly until they separated, a mother who eventually died from complications due to alcohol abuse. You don't need a lot of psychology to know that when he says marriage isn't for him, he means it—not with a background like that." She looked at Bettina and raised her hands in a gesture of helplessness. "I want marriage, I want—"

"Hey!" Ben's shaggy blond head poked through the kitchen door. "Are you two going to gab in here all afternoon? C'mon—we've got the Trivial Pursuit game set up. Van, you lucky girl, you get to play with me. I convinced Shane that principals have more trivial knowledge jammed into their heads than librarians do." He grinned. "And he believed me. Let's get playing—we've got a bet riding on the outcome. Loser buys tickets to the next Jets hockey game."

"Oh?" Bettina raised a fine, dark eyebrow. "And what's in it for us?"

"A chance to shine. What more d'you want?"

"IT'S TIME WE WERE OFF, Bets," Ben said lazily, looking at his watch.

Bettina nodded reluctantly. "I suppose it is, although I hate to go. It's so warm and cozy here." She smiled. "We've had a wonderful time. Thanks for having us."

Vanessa waved a hand dismissingly. "It wouldn't be Christmas without you."

"By the way, Marcie." Bettina turned to the girl. "Are you still coming to spend New Year's Eve with Haili while Ben and I go out?"

"Yeah, sure. Should I spent the night?"

"It's probably best." Bettina nodded. "We'll probably be quite late. Is that all right with you, Van?"

"Of course. Are you still going to Carla's party?"

"Yes—they're usually a lot of fun," Bettina added. "Shane—she invited you as well. Are you going?"

Shane shook his head. "I've already made other plans."

Other plans with whom? Vanessa wondered. Jealousy stabbed viciously at her insides as she struggled to hide her disappointment.

"Well, anyway, it's time we were going," Bettina said with a quick sympathetic look at Vanessa. She got to her feet. "Come on, kidling." She beckoned to Haili. "Let's go."

Shane left shortly afterward giving Cora and Marcie each a fond kiss on the cheek before departing.

"It's been one of the best Christmas Days I've ever had," he said, holding Cora's hand in his. "Thank you for having me."

Cora squeezed his hand warmly. "Your being here added a lot to the day," she said. "We were glad to have you. Come again soon."

"I will." He dropped another kiss on her cheek. "See you soon," he said with a little wave as he followed Vanessa to the door.

Vanessa waited with him in the front hall as he put on his coat, wondering when she would see him again. It won't be New Year's Eve, she thought, her stomach twisting with jealousy.

"You know," he said suddenly, his voice low, "I don't want to leave." He took her face in his hands and kissed her slowly. "What I want to do," he murmured, his breath warm on her lips, "is take you upstairs and make love to you, over and over again. A perfect way to end a perfect day." He kissed her again, his mouth hard and demanding the passion she willingly gave. Abruptly, he broke away.

"I've got to go," he muttered tightly. "While I still can." He touched a finger to her lips, his smile brooding. "Don't make me wait much longer," he said, turning to open the door. "See you soon." With a wave, he was gone into the cold night.

Vanessa shut the door behind him, leaning against it for a moment, giving herself time to recover. See you soon, he'd said. How soon? Tomorrow? The next day? Next week? She locked the door and turned away.

CHAPTER SEVEN

"I CAN PHONE IDA and tell her I'm staying home tonight, if you'd rather." There was worry in Cora's eyes as she looked at Vanessa sitting beside her on the living-room couch. "I don't mind, dear."

"Don't be silly, Gran. I'm perfectly all right. Go ahead, have fun. Don't disappoint Mrs. Corbett—you know she's looking forward to you spending the night. It's no big deal to be alone on New Year's Eve. Besides, I can always change my mind and go to Carla's party later on if I want."

"Are you sure?"

"Absolutely." Vanessa was adamant. "I'm going to have a nice, leisurely evening. I'm looking forward to it."

Cora sighed. "I was so sure you'd be going out with Shane tonight."

"Well, I'm not. And it doesn't matter, Gran. We're just friends." The words came out flatter than she would have liked.

"Then maybe you're not trying hard enough, Vanessa."

Vanessa's eyebrows shot up in surprise. "Gran—I'm trying *very* hard—to keep things friendly." She frowned a bit, speaking honestly. "It would be very easy to become his—his lover, but..." She sighed and rubbed at the line cutting her brow. "He's made it very plain on more than one occasion that he has no intention of ever getting married, Gran. And I—I love him. Sooner or later, I'd need that kind of commitment from him."

"It's entirely possible he'll change his mind. He won't be the first confirmed bachelor to do so."

Vanessa shook her head. "I don't think so, Gran. Besides, I'm not so sure I'd be the woman to do it. I know he's attracted to me, but—" She sighed again. "I think I'm as much a challenge to him as anything. Once that's gone—well, I think he'd be gone, too." She looked at her grandmother, her eyes clouding. "It's going to hurt so much, Gran," she whispered.

"Vanessa—" Cora frowned and shook her head. "This doesn't sound like you at all. I've never seen you so—so pessimistic. If you want the man, then go after him. Put your trust in love—it can sway the most stubborn of hearts. And if things don't work out, well, you'll have the memories." She patted Vanessa's hand and smiled affectionately. "It may seem like small consolation now, but there comes a time when memories are your most treasured possessions. Trust me, dear. Don't hide from life—take what it has to offer. Now—the pep talk's over. Call a cab for me, will you please, while I get my overnight case."

"Will do. And Gran—" Vanessa gave Cora a loving hug. "You're the best."

The house seemed unnaturally quiet after Cora left. Vanessa wandered restlessly from room to room. Maybe she should have gone to the party after all, she thought, but shook her head at the idea. Carla's parties were big affairs, with wall-to-wall people and loud music. Vanessa knew she would end up standing in some corner, bored, as people milled around drinking too much, becoming louder and sillier as the evening progressed. And come midnight, she would slip away somewhere to avoid the exchange of sloppy New Year kisses. No, she thought grimacing, I'm just as well off staying home.

A bath failed to relax her and she got out of the tub after a few minutes, dressing in a fleecy yellow sweatshirt and comfortable old jeans. After tugging a comb through her hair, she went back downstairs, determined to relax in front of the fire with a book and a glass of wine.

The book failed to hold her attention and she let it slide from her hands onto the floor beside her as she sipped her wine, staring into the flickering flames.

Where was Shane tonight? she wondered. More importantly, who was he with? The thought of him with another woman, as he undoubtedly was, was painful. Who was she? Someone glamorous, Vanessa was sure, someone who wouldn't have any qualms about going to bed with him when the evening was over. Picking up the poker, she jabbed morosely at the logs burning in the fireplace, sending a shower of sparks up the chimney.

The doorbell sounded suddenly. Startled, Vanessa spilled a few drops of wine from the glass she was raising to her lips. Licking the drops from her fingers, she got up, wondering who could possibly be at the door. Turning on the porch light, she peered cautiously outside. Eyes widening in surprise, she stepped back and flung open the door.

"Shane!" she said in pleased surprise.

"Hi." He smiled crookedly, arms cradling a bulk under his parka as he came inside, bringing a rush of cold air with him. "I brought someone to see you," he said, opening his zipper. Bright black eyes looked at her and a small furry body wriggled ecstatically.

Vanessa took the puppy into her arms, laughing delightedly as the fluffy animal swiped at her hands. "Isn't she beautiful?" Vanessa smiled at Shane, hiding none of the pleasure she felt at his unexpected arrival.

"I was hoping you'd be home," he said, shrugging off his parka. "If not, I was going to brave Carla's party and see if you were there."

"What happened to your date for the evening—it was a date, wasn't it?" Vanessa asked, leading the way into the living room. Still holding the puppy, she sat down on the couch, striving for a nonchalance she was far from feeling.

Shane sat on the couch beside her, fingers stroking the dog gently. "I cancelled," he said, his eyes holding hers. "I phoned and explained that it was only fair to tell her that there was someone else I would rather spend the evening with."

Pleasure rushed through Vanessa. "With Sasha?" she murmured, looking down at the dog.

"No, Vanessa. With you." Curling a finger under her chin, he lifted her head and kissed her softly. "Is that all right with you?"

Smiling happily, she nodded.

"Great. Listen—I've got an idea."

"What?"

"There's a full moon tonight," he began. "And the sky is perfectly clear. It's cold, but calm. Would you like to go cross-country skiing?"

"Skiing! At night? Shane, I'm—" She stopped and grinned suddenly. "Actually, it sounds wonderful. Where?"

"At my place—along the creek. It's great terrain for skiing."

"Okay. Just give me a few minutes to get ready." She put the puppy on the floor and stood up. "Oh, could you phone Gran for me and let her know just in case she calls later? I don't want her to worry. The number is in the address book beside the phone, under Ida Corbett. I won't be long," she called over her shoulder.

She was ready in less than ten minutes, dressed in a silver-gray ski suit. After propping her skis against the wall beside the door, she pulled on a bright blue toque and tied a matching scarf around her neck.

"You take the dog and I'll get the skis," Shane said. "And don't forget your key. Oh, by the way, Cora said to tell you to have a good time." He zipped up his parka and reached for the skis. "Ready?"

VANESSA STRAIGHTENED UP from fastening her skis and jammed her numb hands back into her mittens. "I'm ready," she said. "And frozen. Whose idea was this, anyway?"

"Yours, I think." Shane grinned, rubbing his hands together briskly. "We don't have to go, you know."

"We've come this far. We might as well go for it. Besides, it's so incredibly beautiful—the sky is so clear. It might be worth the loss of a few appendages to frostbite." She pulled her scarf up to cover her nose and mouth. "Ready?"

"Just a sec. See if Sasha's all right, will you?" Shane had decided the tiny puppy was too young to run beside them and had put her in a knapsack on his back. Her furry, bright-eyed face poked out through the opening, pink tongue lapping as Vanessa gave her a pat.

"She looks quite comfortable," Vanessa said. "And warm, which is more than I can say for myself. Let's get moving before I freeze to the spot."

"Okay, follow me." Shane grabbed his ski poles and pushed off.

Vanessa fitted her skis into his parallel tracks, gliding easily along behind him. Once into the rhythm, she looked around with a pleasure even the intense cold couldn't mar.

The moon, a cold, glowing orb, pierced the darkness, throwing sharp, stretching shadows across the snow-covered creek. Minute snow crystals glittered like scattered diamond dust. The air was sharp and cold, silent except for the swishing thrust of their skis.

Shane slowed to a stop around one curve where the creek widened to a grain field sloping gently down to the edge. "Okay?" he asked, turning his head toward her.

"Fine," she answered, her breath coming through her scarf in white puffs as she stopped immediately behind him. "Can we keep going?"

"If you want. But not too much farther—we still have to go back, remember."

Shane dug his poles in the snow, took a few gliding strides and then stopped abruptly, looking up over the field. He held up a hand, cautioning her to silence.

"What is it?" she whispered.

"What do you see?" he asked, gesturing.

Puzzled, Vanessa looked up over the moon-bright field. "Hay bales?" she asked, squinting. "No—wait... Are those deer?"

Shane nodded. "They know we're here," he said. "They're watching. They must be feeding on the stubble— the wind would blow most of the snow from the center of the field. During the day, they probably hide in the trees along the river."

"Poor things," Vanessa said. "Winter must be hard on them."

"As long as they have food, they're fine," Shane said.

"I suppose. But still..." Vanessa shivered, suddenly feeling the cold. "As much as I'm enjoying this, I think maybe we'd better head back."

"That's probably a good idea," Shane agreed readily. "The thought of curling up in front of the fireplace is suddenly very appealing."

"With a hot cup of cocoa," Vanessa said as she turned around, careful not to tangle her skis.

"How about a glass of champagne instead? I brought a bottle along. It is New Year's Eve, after all."

"That sounds great." Curling up in front of a roaring fire with Shane and a bottle of champagne, she thought with a rush of excitement. It sounded fantastic. And if he reached for her... She shivered, not from cold, but from a touch of apprehension.

When they got back they removed their skis and propped them against the side of the house. Shane took the puppy from the knapsack and she scampered around, stopping for a roll in the snow. Vanessa pulled the scarf from her face and rubbed her mittens over the dampness around her mouth, taking one last look at the night sky.

"Oh, look, Shane," she said softly. "Northern lights."

Shane looked up, putting an arm around her shoulders and pulling her close to him.

Pale luminous veils of green and violet shimmered beneath the stars, stretching, shrinking, constantly shifting across the sky. As they watched, distant church bells pealed through the still, frigid air.

"It's midnight," Shane said. He turned her to face him. "Happy New Year, Vanessa," he murmured, his face cut deep by moon shadows.

"Happy New Year, Shane." Vanessa touched her cold lips to his, feeling them warm instantly. His kiss was brief and hard.

"Let's go in," he said, "and start that fire."

Vanessa nodded and followed him inside, but as far as she was concerned, the fire had been started long ago.

"You've been painting," Vanessa commented, looking around the living room as Shane knelt in front of the fireplace, carefully stacking kindling in the grate. The creamy almond color was a warm contrast to the gleaming woodwork.

"I had someone come out last week to do it," Shane said, striking a match and holding it to crumbled newspaper. Flames licked eagerly, shooting up the chimney.

"It looks good," Vanessa approved. He had also added a big comfortable-looking couch, which faced the fireplace, and a plush blue and cream-colored area rug. There was a colorful clutter of cushions scattered on the floor near the hearth. "So does the furniture, sparse as it is."

"It's a start," Shane said. "The couch will eventually go in the den. I've been sleeping on it the past couple of nights—it folds down into a bed." He smiled at the puppy as she crept close to the fire and peered cautiously at the flames. As he ruffled the fur around her ears, she grabbed at his hand and Vanessa laughed as they tussled playfully.

Moving closer to the fire, Vanessa sat cross-legged on the edge of the rug, holding her hands out to the heat. Shane disappeared into the kitchen, the dog scampering after him, claws clicking on the wooden floor. He returned carrying a bottle of champagne, popped the cork and poured the bubbling golden liquid into two long-stemmed crystal flute glasses. Handing her one, he sat beside her, his thigh resting comfortably against hers.

The dog flopped down in front of them, chewed on the end of Shane's thick woolen sock for a moment, jumping up in surprise as a log popped in the fireplace. Shane and Vanessa laughed as the puppy regarded the flames suspiciously, her ears pointed sharply forward. Turning around, she yawned with a little squeak, lay down and closed her eyes.

"Happy New Year again," Shane said, his eyes smiling into hers as he touched his glass to hers.

"Happy New Year," Vanessa murmured. She took a sip of champagne. "Mm, my favorite drink." She took another sip. She was feeling so much more comfortable than she had thought was possible, relaxed and warming after skiing in the cold, brisk nighttime air. The desire she felt for Shane, the anticipation of the kisses she knew would come, simmered in her without urgency. For now, it was enough to sit close, sharing the moment. She would not worry about what might happen later, but would take each moment as it came and do what felt right to her.

"The coals are about right for popcorn," Shane said, after a few minutes of shared silence. "I can make some if you'd like."

"Champagne and popcorn," Vanessa said. "It sounds delicious. I'd love some."

Shane got lazily to his feet and went to the kitchen, returning quickly. Kneeling in front of the fire, he put the foil-covered aluminum plate over the coals, holding it by the handle.

"Shake it hard," Vanessa ordered playfully, leaning forward to stroke the sleeping puppy. "I hate burned popcorn."

"Yes, ma'am." Shane grinned at her and gave the pan an obliging shake.

Vanessa sipped her champagne, savoring the dry, bubbly taste. She twisted around until she was lying curled on her side, propping her head up on one hand. Taking another swallow of champagne, she studied Shane's partially averted face, watching the firelight flicker on the chiseled curve of his cheek.

I love him so much, she thought with a strong rush of feeling, *and he cares for me, I know he does.* Maybe it wasn't love he felt, but she'd be crazy to think that he simply saw her as a challenge, someone he wanted a short-term affair with. She had to mean more to him than that, she realized. She looked down at her drink, running a finger around the rim of her glass. He liked her, wanted to be with her—wasn't tonight proof enough of that?

Shane took the aluminum pan from the fire and pulled back the foil, revealing a mound of fragrant popcorn. "Vanessa? Hey—wake up. Popcorn's ready." He put the pan down on the floor between them. "What were you thinking about, anyway?" he asked, taking the bottle of champagne and topping off their glasses.

Vanessa smiled at him. "About how much I've enjoyed tonight. And how glad I am to be here with you."

"The feeling is mutual, lovely lady," he said gruffly.

"I was also thinking," she continued, her lashes sweeping down then up again as she looked at him directly, "how much I'd like to kiss you." She heard his sudden intake of breath, saw desire glaze his eyes.

"I'm waiting," he said huskily.

Vanessa slowly pushed herself up until she was sitting on her knees in front of him. Feeling warm, sensuously desired, she put her hands on his shoulders and leaned forward, kissing him lightly on the forehead, his cheeks, around the jut of his jaw to the softness of his mouth. Delicately she darted her tongue over the parting of his lips and then pulled back suddenly, smiling at him. "There," she said.

"Call that a kiss?" he asked, his voice low and soft.

Her fingers stroked the back of his neck. "Are you complaining?"

"Yeah," he murmured, his eyes half closed. He wrapped a lock of her hair around his finger and tugged gently. "Try it again," he demanded, his eyes soft and irresistibly sexy.

Vanessa's fingers raked through his gleaming tumble of curls, tightening as she leaned forward and kissed him with all the passion she felt.

Shane pulled away with a groan. "You're driving me wild, woman," he muttered. "I want you so damned bad."

Vanessa ran her hands over his shoulders, pressing her palms hard against his muscled back. "So what are you waiting for?" she whispered. She felt his sharp intake of breath, felt his muscles tense.

His thumbs stroked the hair back from her forehead as his eyes searched hers. "Are you sure, Vanessa?"

She took one of his hands and held it to her cheek, smiling at him with all the love she felt. "Oh, yes," she whispered. "I'm sure."

Shane let out a deep breath and pulled her into his arms, pressing her head to his shoulder, his fingers stroking the nape of her neck through her hair. She raised her face and kissed softly along the jut of his jaw, one hand slipping beneath his sweater to rest above his thudding heart.

"Vanessa," he groaned, his arms tightening as their bodies pressed hard against each other. "I—" He stopped, his mouth covering hers with hard urgency. His hands tugged at her clothes until they found her breasts, stroking, kneading, arousing her further with every caress. Lost to his touch, she returned his passion with uncurbed abandon.

SHANE HELD HER CLOSE in his sleep, his hips curving snugly against hers as they shared the soft, comfortable mattress of the sofa bed, warm beneath a satin-covered duvet. Vanessa lay, drowsily content, staring into the fire, feeling his breath, warm and soft, stirring her hair.

Their lovemaking had been perfect, beautiful and yet wildly passionate, everything she had known it would be and so much more.

He cared for her, she thought with sleepy certainty. Maybe he didn't love her yet, but there was time, time to let him know of her love for him and, she hoped, time to convince him that they belonged together. Tonight, for the first time, she was sure that they had a future together.

Slowly she turned in his arms until she was facing him, her breath mingling softly with his. She stroked the tumble of curls from his forehead and ran an insistent hand over his ribs to the curve of his hips. "I love you so much," she whispered and pressed her lips to his as he awakened to her rising passion. They made love again, slowly this time, with a passionate tenderness that left her trembling. Tears of joy slid down her cheeks and he kissed them away, holding her close in his arms. As she drifted off to sleep, he lay awake, staring into corners that darkened as the fire slowly faded and died.

When she awoke again, she was alone in the tumble of blankets. New flames crackled brightly in the fireplace and a winter's soft dawn lightened the room.

Stretching languorously and then curling back into a ball, Vanessa closed her eyes again, feeling disappointed that Shane was no longer beside her. She would have loved to awaken in his arms, warm and cuddled, perhaps make love again. Last night had been incredibly beautiful, she thought drowsily. For all the passion that had flared between them, there had been an underlying tenderness to Shane's touch. Thinking about it, Vanessa smiled with strengthening optimism. Surely their relationship could only grow from this.

She heard Shane come back into the room. Opening her eyes, she smiled at him. "There you are," she said. "I hope that's coffee you're carrying."

"It is."

"Mine?"

"Yep—I had mine while you were still sleeping the sleep of the innocent."

She stretched luxuriously, smiling at the night's memories. "Not so innocent," she murmured.

Shane smiled. "No—delightfully wanton would be a more apt description." He sat down on the edge of the bed, putting a mug of coffee on the floor. Cupping her head in his hands, he thumbed the hair back from her forehead, smiling softly. "Good morning," he murmured. He kissed each cheek, then touched his lips to hers. "Last night was wonderful," he said, his eyes soft. "You, lovely lady, are fantastic."

Vanessa wrapped her arms around his neck, burying her face in his shoulder, breathing deeply his warm, male scent and trembling with a rush of strong feeling for him. "I love you so much," she whispered, her voice trembling.

She felt him stiffen slightly, then he held her close, kissing the top of her head. Releasing her suddenly, he picked up the coffee mug and handed it to her. "Drink up," he commanded gently. "Then get dressed. I've got to go let the dog in." After one last lingering look through expressionless eyes, he got to his feet and left the room.

Vanessa sat up quickly, reaching for clothes. Hadn't he heard what she had unwittingly confessed, or was he choosing to ignore it? He must have heard, she thought and felt a sharp stab of disappointment, worried because he had grown suddenly distant and hadn't responded. She finished dressing and stood by the fire, drinking her lukewarm coffee.

She glanced at him when he came back into the room, followed closely by the puppy, but could read nothing in his expression. Looking away quickly, she took another swallow of coffee as the dog hurried eagerly toward her. Kneeling down, she petted the exuberant puppy, watching Shane out of the corner of her eye as he folded up the sofa bed. Maybe she was being overly anxious, but she sensed something different.

Straightening up, she moved to help him fold the bedding. "Shane—is something wrong?"

He turned and looked at her, brows arching over heavy-lidded eyes. "Wrong? Of course not." He dropped the pillow he had been holding and pulled her into his arms. Cupping the back of her head, he kissed her gently. "Is that better?" He smiled.

It was, for a moment, but when he released her to finish putting things away, the feeling of unease started again.

Before long they were in the car heading back to the city. It was becoming obvious to her that Shane had chosen to ignore her declaration of love, that he didn't want to complicate their relationship with unwanted emotions. They should talk about it, she knew, but when she tried to broach the subject, the words stuck in her throat. She was afraid to hear what he might say, to listen to his apologies for not returning her feelings, afraid of the sympathy she would see in his eyes. She followed his lead and they talked only of unimportant things.

"I'll help you with your skis," he said as he stopped the car in front of her house.

Vanessa nodded, giving Sasha a final pat as she got out of the car. Shane unfastened her skis from the rack on the trunk of his car.

"There," he said, tucking them under his arm. "Got your key?"

Vanessa fished it from her pocket. "Right here." She led the way up the sidewalk. "Just prop the skis against the wall," she said as she opened the door. "I'll put them away later. Would you like some breakfast?" she asked, hoping fervently that he would stay.

He hesitated. "No—no, thanks," he said. "I've got something planned for this afternoon and it's almost eleven already. I'd better be going."

Vanessa hid her disappointment. Nothing this morning was turning out like it should.

"Vanessa—" He put his hands on her shoulders. "I—" He stopped with a little shake of his head. "I'll call you." He kissed her softly. "See you," he said, with a funny little smile, then he was gone.

Tears sprung to Vanessa's eyes. Last night had been so beautiful—how could it have turned into this? Shane had been embarrassed by her declaration of love, concerned that she would start demanding more from the relationship than he wanted to give. She turned away from the door and trudged wearily up the stairs to her room. I shouldn't have said anything, she thought, I should have pretended it was just a physical thing for me as well. But how long could she have denied the love she felt?

The rest of the day passed in a blur. First Cora then Marcie came home and after lunch friends began to call, making their New Year's Day rounds. There was little time to brood.

After a late supper, she lay alone in her room, staring at the ceiling. How long would it be before Shane called? Would he ever call again? Of course he will, she assured herself, fighting the niggling feeling that maybe he'd gotten what he wanted from her and now just wanted to extricate himself from a relationship that threatened to become sticky with unwanted emotions. In spite of her growing lack of confidence, she couldn't really believe that, not after the friendship they'd built up. Shane might be skittish about love and the commitment it entailed, but he wasn't a user. Perhaps he just needed time to come to grips with the fact that she was in love with him. Vanessa sighed and rubbed a hand across her brow. Still, she thought, it wasn't fair of him to leave her with these doubts and worries.

I'll call him, she thought, rolling to her side and reaching for the phone, and we can talk it out. Quickly she dialed his number, her stomach clenching nervously as his phone began to ring. She heard a click and then his voice, an impersonal recorded message on his answering machine.

"It's Vanessa, Shane," she said diffidently into the receiver. "Please call me. I really need to talk to you." With a little sigh, she hung up. All she could do now was wait.

CHAPTER EIGHT

SHANE HADN'T RETURNED her call by the time school started again. Fighting a rising despair, Vanessa tried to convince herself that there had to be a good reason behind his actions, but she knew she was fooling herself. Hard as it was, she had to admit to herself that she had been wrong about Shane all along. What else could it be? Her despair began to turn into a grim kind of anger and she began to prepare herself to confront him after his session with Tommy.

As she sat at her desk on the first Tuesday back after the holidays, leafing blindly through a magazine, Bettina came into the office. She'd missed her the day before in all the commotion.

"Hi, Van. How's it going?" she asked cheerfully, sitting on a chair in front of the desk. Crossing her long, slim legs, she smoothed her skirt over her knees.

"Fine, thanks." Vanessa looked up and forced a smile. "Glad to be back?"

"Oh, yes—sure. Nose to the grindstone; no more holidays till the end of March—who wouldn't be glad?" She looked closely at Vanessa. "Okay, Van, let's have it."

"Have what?"

"What's happened between you and Shane?"

"What makes you think something has?" Vanessa prevaricated.

"Your face, for one thing," Bettina said bluntly. "I haven't seen you looking so pale and withdrawn since—well, in a long time. Also, I have a message from Shane saying he's sorry but he won't be able to come to the school to work with Tommy any longer. Not that he's abandoning him,'' Bettina added. ''Apparently he's arranged with Mrs. Hawkes to see Tommy after school at the public library. What's up, Van?'' she asked, her voice softly sympathetic.

''What's up,'' Vanessa began bitterly, ''is that I was right about Shane at the beginning. He belongs to the use 'em and lose 'em club.''

Bettina shook her head. ''No, Vanessa. I can't believe that for a second.''

''Oh, yeah? Then you explain it to me.'' Vanessa looked down at her hands. ''We—we made love for the first time on New Year's Eve,'' she said in a low voice. ''After a moonlit ski, and champagne in front of the fireplace. It was wonderful, Bettina—exquisitely beautiful.'' She looked up, her eyes dull and troubled. ''The next morning I told him I loved him. It spooked him, I guess. He drove me home and I haven't seen or heard from him since. That was almost a week ago, Bettina. He doesn't even bother to return my calls. And now you tell me—'' She stopped and brushed angrily at the tears that threatened to fall. ''Did I get suckered in or what?''

Bettina was frowning. ''There must be so some explanation, Van. There *has* to be.''

Vanessa sighed wearily. ''He's afraid,'' she said flatly. ''Afraid I'll start demanding some kind of commitment from him. He cleared out before things could get sticky.'' She looked at Bettina and attempted to smile. ''I sure know how to pick them, don't I?''

Bettina held up her hands in a gesture of helplessness. ''I'm sorry, Van—you deserve better. What are you going to do now?''

Vanessa glanced at the clock on the wall. ''I'm going to take my first class and then I'm going to go over to his place and—and confront him. If he doesn't want my love—fine. I can learn to live with it. But he's going to have to tell me to my face.''

VANESSA MANAGED TO SMILE at the elderly man sharing the elevator with her, but looked away before he could speak, wanting to keep her mind on what she was going to say to Shane.

What could she say to him, but let him know how much he had hurt her? As painful as it was, she had to acknowledge that there could be nothing further between them. Obviously he didn't want her love, and there was no way she would continue to see a man who had treated her so badly. The elevator stopped and she stepped off, tightening the hold on her anger. It was all that would get her through this confrontation.

It was all for nothing. Shane wasn't home. Vanessa pressed the doorbell futilely in frustration. She opened her purse, hunting for a scrap of paper, finally tearing out one of her checks and scribbling a hurried note on the back. We have to talk, she wrote. You owe me that much. She folded the paper, slipped it under his door and left.

TOMMY CAME DOWN to the library that afternoon to see her. "Look Ms Evans," he said, thrusting a photograph at her. "It's a picture of me an' my dog, Wolf. Mr. Wilder took it so I could show everyone."

Vanessa looked at the picture of Tommy clutching a small brown dog that looked more cocker spaniel than wolf. "He's beautiful, Tommy," she said as she handed back the picture. "You must be very glad to have him."

"Yeah." Tommy nodded vigorously as he tucked the picture into the back pocket of his jeans. "An' I have to take him for a walk two times a day an' make sure he has food an' water. Mr. Wilder buys the food," he added.

"Have you seen Mr. Wilder lately?" she asked, keeping her tone casual.

"Yeah, sure. Last night. He took me an' my mom out for supper. We had pizza and' I had pep—pep'roni with mushrooms. He said he's gotta go away for a while, but he'd take me skating when he got back. Is five minutes up yet? Miss Napier said I hadda be back in five minutes."

"Well, then, you'd better be off. Thanks for showing me the picture, Tommy." She smiled at the boy as he hurried out of the library.

So Shane had to go away? Where was he going? She wondered why hadn't he told her? She sighed and wearily rubbed the back of her neck. It just confirmed what she had started to believe. He didn't want anything more to do with her. The rest of the day passed painstakingly slowly, and Vanessa welcomed the sound of the final bell. She drove home pensively, relieved when she finally pulled up to he house. "Gran—I'm home." She dropped her books on the kitchen table and shrugged off her coat, weary from a day of conflicting emotions. She had wavered between anger and despair all day.

"Hello, dear." Cora poked her head into the kitchen. "Come in here," she beckoned. "Something came for you today."

Picking up her coat, Vanessa followed her grandmother into the living room. On the sideboard was a cascading bouquet of colorful flowers carefully arranged in a finely etched brass vase.

"Aren't they gorgeous?" Cora was beaming as she handed Vanessa a small envelope. "They came in that vase—it's a beautiful keepsake."

With trembling fingers, Vanessa opened the envelope. There was no message on the card, just Shane's name scrawled across it in strong, black letters.

"From Shane?" Cora questioned.

Vanessa nodded.

"What does he say—or is it safe to ask?" Cora teased gently.

Vanessa's face felt stiff and unresponsive as she attempted to smile. "He doesn't say anything. He only signed his name."

"Ah, well, I guess he's said it all already."

"Yes, Gran, he has. Only too clearly." Vanessa's voice was grim.

Startled, Cora looked at her. "What's wrong, dear?" she asked in gentle concern.

Vanessa blinked back tears and turned away. "I—I won't be seeing Shane any more, Gran."

"What! But I thought—" Cora stopped and looked at her granddaughter's stiffly held back. "What happened, Vanessa?"

Vanessa shook her head, clenching her hands tightly for control. "I can't talk about it just now, Gran." She turned to Cora and managed a shaky smile. "I'm going to my room," she said. "I need to be alone for a while."

Upstairs in her room, she kicked off her shoes and paced the floor, hugging her arms tight to her chest. Why had Shane sent the flowers? Were they an apology or just a thanks for the memories? He could have said something, she thought. Any kind of message would have been better than nothing.

Why did I have to tell him I loved him? she asked herself as tears coursed down her cheeks. That had to be the reason behind all this. He wanted her as a friend and lover, but not to be in love with him. If she hadn't said those three little words, would he have dropped her like he had? If only— She stopped and shook her head angrily. All the hindsight in the world didn't change the fact that the man she loved didn't want anything more to do with her.

VANESSA STRUGGLED WEARILY out of bed. Snow fell from thick pewter clouds and was whipped around by the cold north wind into hard-packed drifts. Nearly three weeks had passed since she had last seen Shane. From remarks Tommy made, she knew that he was still out of town, keeping in touch with the boy through letters and postcards. Where he had gone, she didn't bother to find out. It would make no difference to the pain and anger churning inside of her.

She showered and dressed, then drank a cup of coffee with Cora, trying to make cheerful small talk, wanting to dispel the worried look she saw in her grandmother's eyes.

"I've got to be going," she said, glancing at the clock on the wall as she swallowed the last of her coffee. She pulled on her boots and jammed her arms into her coat, buttoning it under her chin. Picking up her gloves and purse, she kissed Cora's cheek. "See you tonight, Gran."

"Goodbye, dear. Have a good day." Cora watched her leave, a concerned line evident across her brow.

The roads were slippery with new snow, but not unduly so. Vanessa stopped at a red light, reaching to adjust the volume on the radio. A sudden, violent crash from behind sent her car skidding into the intersection. Her head whipped forward and then back, hitting against the head-rest. Stunned, she sat uncomprehendingly, scarcely hearing the blare of a horn and screech of brakes as another car, traveling through the intersection, rammed into the far side of her car.

The force thrust her hard against the door and her head slammed against the window. The last thing she heard was the sound of breaking glass as she fell into darkness.

LIGHT SEEPED THROUGH her lashes as her eyelids fluttered, trying to open, and the pervasive smell of hospital disinfectant permeated her fogged senses.

"Vanessa."

Dimly she heard her grandmother's voice and struggled to force her eyes open. She was lying on a hospital bed with the curtains pulled around it. Cora stood beside her, holding tight to her hand. Vanessa blinked, focusing her eyes.

"You're in the hospital emergency, dear," Cora explained, her face white and anxious. "You're okay—bruised and shaken, but there's nothing to worry about."

Vanessa started to nod and stopped quickly, wincing at the pain shooting through her head. "Was—was anyone else—'' The words stuck in her throat and she swallowed to ease the dryness.

"No one else was hurt," Cora assured her. "Just a few scratches, that's all." She smoothed Vanessa's hair back from her forehead, her hand soft and cool. "Your head was cut a bit where you hit the window—there'll be a bruise, the doctor said, but the cuts aren't serious." She took a sharp breath. "You're lucky, Vanessa. If that car had hit your side—" Her voice broke off and she tightened her grip on Vanessa's hand, her eyes wide and dark with shock.

Vanessa knew what memories were flooding through her grandmother's mind. "Sit down, Gran," she said, her voice a croaking whisper. "I'm okay—don't worry. It will be fine."

Nodding, Cora sat abruptly, as though her legs would no longer support her. She dropped her head to her hands and let out a shaky breath. After a moment she raised her head and managed to smile. "I'm all right now," she said, turning as she heard someone enter the room.

A woman with soft gray hair and a gentle, lined face pushed aside the curtain surrounding the bed.

"Ah, good—you're awake," she smiled at Vanessa. "I'm Dr. Isabel Storey. I examined you when you came in." She took Vanessa's wrist in hers, feeling for her pulse. "How are you feeling?"

Vanessa managed a bit of a smile. "Not bad."

"Well, it will a few days before you'll start feeling normal again. Still, you're lucky. Nothing's broken—not even your head, although it might feel like it." She smiled warmly. "You'll probably grow a goose egg, and you'll have a king-size headache, but there's no fracture." She put Vanessa's hand down, patting it gently. Turning to Cora, she asked abruptly. "How are you doing, Mrs. Evans?"

"I'm all right now, thank you." Cora's voice was stronger and the color was coming back to her face. "It was a shock."

Dr. Storey eyed her closely then nodded. "Good. We're going to take your granddaughter to a private room now— I think it best she stay overnight. Why don't you go up with her and once she's settled, get yourself home. Relax—take a nap. Everything will be okay here." She put a hand on Cora's shoulder and squeezed gently. "Take care of yourself now."

"Will do. Thank you, doctor."

Vanessa succumbed to painkillers and a darkened, quiet room, sleeping the afternoon away. She picked listlessly at her supper, finally pushing the tray away with a grimace of disgust. Her head ached and the left side of her body was beginning to bruise and stiffen.

Cora came for an evening visit, accompanied by an anxious Marcie. Bettina arrived shortly after, carrying a big basket of fruit from the staff of the school and assurances that she'd managed to obtain a good substitute for Vanessa's classes.

As much as she enjoyed the company, Vanessa felt relieved when they finally left. It was too much of an effort to carry on a conversation. She accepted another painkiller from the nurse and fell into numbing sleep immediately.

Morning brought the full brunt of pain. Her head hurt the most, throbbing with dull, incessant pain. After breakfast, she forced herself out of bed to wash and change into one of the nightgowns Cora had brought for her, tying her deep-red velour robe over top. Then she gingerly brushed her hair, pulling a lock forward to hide the swelling on her temple.

Groaning softly at the soreness in her muscles, she eased herself onto the bed, raising the mattress to a sitting position. Straightening the robe over her legs, she leaned back against the pillow, closing her eyes and holding a hand against her aching head.

"Vanessa."

She stiffened. Her eyes flew open and she stared at Shane standing just inside the doorway to her room, bouquet of pink roses in hand.

"What do you want?" she demanded in a thin whisper.

"I came to see you," he said, coming closer to the bed. His eyes were narrow with concern as they swept over her pale face. "How are you?" he asked, putting the roses on the table at the foot of her bed.

"Oh, fine. How are you?" Her voice was laced with sarcasm. "What do you care?"

He took a step closer, a sharp line cutting his brow. "I do care, Vanessa. I—"

"Leave me alone, Shane," she said, cutting him off. "Go away."

"I want to talk," he said.

"Talk?" Her voice rose sharply. "It's about three weeks too late for a talk. Just get away from me."

"No," he said firmly, taking one of her hands in his. "Not until we've talked about—things."

Anger twisted in her stomach and she pulled her hand from his. "I don't want to talk to you, not now, not ever." Her voice cracked. "Get out of my life, Shane Wilder. Stay out of my life!"

Shane's face was still and inscrutable. He moved as though to touch her.

"No!" Pain shot through her body as she jerked away from his hand, and she cried out. She put a hand to her head and turned away from him as tears of pain and anger coursed hotly down her face. "Leave me alone," she said through gritted teeth. "Just—stay away from me."

Shane let out a harsh breath, his voice tight when he spoke again. "I can see you're in no condition to talk to me. I'll go, Vanessa—for now. We'll talk when you're able." For a fleeting moment, his hand rested on her shoulder and he turned to walk away.

Vanessa sat up and snatched up the flowers he had left, throwing them at his retreating back. Whimpering from the pain, she fell back against the pillow, covering her face with her hands as sobs tore from her throat.

Weakened from the accident, Vanessa could no longer find the strength to fight the pain and sense of betrayal Shane had left her with. When she returned home from the hospital, she slipped into a lethargic state of emotional numbness, spending her days laying in her darkened room with the radio a soft blur of background noise.

Cora came up to her room late one morning carrying a tray. She put it down on the night table beside Vanessa's bed, looking down on her sleeping granddaughter with a worried frown. She went to the windows and tugged open the curtains. Sunlight struggled through high, rippled clouds and lightened the room. Bright rainbows from the crystal butterfly swaying in the window pirouetted around the room.

"Wake up, Vanessa," Cora said gently, coming back to the bed. "I brought you some tea and toast, and a nice soft-boiled egg, if you can manage it."

Vanessa stirred and yawned, wincing a bit as her still-sore muscles protested. "You shouldn't have, Gran," she said guiltily, sitting up in bed. "I'd have come down when I woke up."

"It's taking you longer and longer to wake up each morning," Cora said. She moved the tray from the night table and laid it across Vanessa's lap. "Eat up now," she ordered, pulling the wicker stool from behind the silk screen and sitting on it beside the bed.

Vanessa took a grateful swallow of hot, strong tea then picked up a piece of toast, nibbling at it without appetite.

"I'm worried about you, Vanessa," Cora said in her forthright manner. "It's more than just bumps and bruises causing you to behave like this."

Frowning, Vanessa put down the toast. "Gran—I don't want to talk about it."

"Well, I think it's about time that you did," Cora said firmly. "I know it's to do with Shane, and I know you're refusing to talk to him about it. Why?"

"He's got nothing to say that I want to hear," Vanessa said, her face set.

"Doesn't he? I think you're wrong, dear. And you owe it to yourself to find out."

Vanessa shook her head wearily. "I don't want to hear his excuses, Gran. He's made it clear enough that he doesn't want me or—or love me." She swallowed and blinked back unwelcome tears. "I don't need to hear the reasons."

"I think you're making a mistake, Vanessa. And even if you're not—well, I think you need to talk to him about it or you're going to be a long time in healing emotionally. Give yourself a day or two, then go talk to him," she pleaded gently. "Will you, dear? For me?"

Vanessa sighed and nodded reluctantly. She'd do it for Cora.

THREE DAYS AFTER her talk with Cora, Vanessa woke early, feeling stronger than she had since the accident. She got up with hardly a twinge of protest from her muscles and went to shower, relishing the hot, reviving spray.

She dried her hair, putting a soft wave over the dull, yellowing bruise on her temple, and applied makeup lightly. After dressing in dark-gray woolen slacks and a deep-red angora sweater, she went downstairs.

Cora was in the kitchen drying the breakfast dishes she and Marcie had used. "Good morning, dear," she said. "You look much better this morning."

"I feel better, Gran," Vanessa said, enjoying the rich aroma of the coffee as she poured herself a cup. "I'm not nearly as stiff and sore as I was." She sat down at the table, stirring milk into her coffee. "I'm going to see Shane today," she said decidedly.

Cora turned from putting dishes into the cupboard. "I'm glad to hear that," she smiled approvingly. "Oh—he's been moving into his house over this past week. He'll probably be out there."

"How do you know?" Vanessa asked in surprise.

"He phoned and told me," Cora said casually, picking up a handful of flatware from the drain board. "We've been keeping in touch. He wanted to know how you were doing."

"What did you tell him?"

"That you were sore and hurting," Cora answered calmly. "Nothing more nor less than the truth. Now—can I fix you something to eat before you leave?"

Vanessa felt her stomach tighten. "No, thank you, Gran." She put down her coffee cup and took a deep breath. "I'm going to leave right now while I've still got the nerve."

Ben and Bettina had dropped off their second car the night before, assuring Vanessa that they could easily do without it until her insurance claim was settled and she could buy a new one.

Vanessa gripped the steering wheel tightly, her driving slow and overcautious, as she constantly checked the rear-view mirror. By the time she'd reached the city limits, she was taut with nervousness both from the strain of driving and the thought of seeing Shane.

The temptation to turn around and go home was great, but she fought it. Hard as it might be to face Shane, she was going to go through with it. She was determined to get the explanation and apology owed her. Maybe then she could harden her heart enough to deaden the pain and get on with her life, empty as it was going to be. She turned from the highway onto the tree-lined drive leading to his house.

Parking the car beside his, she stayed where she was for a few moments, looking around. It was a clear day. Wispy fingers of fog had laid thick white crystals of frost on the gray branches and golden grasses. Traces lingered above the creek and among the trees, blurring the landscape.

I can still leave, Vanessa thought as her stomach twisted with a rush of panic. He wouldn't have recognized the car if he was looking outside. He wouldn't know it was her. She fought the urge to flee as she opened the car door and stepped out into the soft moist air. Going quickly to the door, she knocked loudly while she still had the nerve.

Shane opened the door almost immediately. For a moment his face reflected surprise, but then it settled into impassive lines. "Vanessa," he said, his voice polite and expressionless. "Please—come in."

"Thank you," Vanessa murmured, stepping inside. She glanced at him as he closed the door behind her. He was wearing faded jeans and a black sweatshirt, his feet bare inside a pair of worn moccasins. She looked hurriedly away as he turned back to her.

"Here—give me your coat."

Vanessa shrugged her jacket into his waiting hands. Where should she start? What should she say? "Are you all moved in?" she asked, her eyes darting restlessly around the kitchen with its gleaming new appliances.

"Just about," he answered. "I was just unpacking books in the den."

Sasha trotted into the room, stopping with ears cocked to peer brightly at Vanessa.

"She's getting big," Vanessa said, bending down and holding out a hand. "Hi, Sasha—come here, girl." I want to leave, she thought with growing doubt and nervousness. "Good girl," she murmured as the puppy ran toward her, rear end wriggling in ecstasy as she licked at Vanessa's hand. At least one of them is glad to see me, she thought, rubbing the thick ruff on the back of the dog's neck. As she stood up, she glanced at Shane's impassive face.

"Vanessa..." He took her by the shoulders and turned her to face him, searching her still face with cautious eyes. "I'm glad you came," he said. He touched one hand to the faint bruise on her temple, his eyes darkening. "I hurt you," he whispered huskily. "I'm sorry."

Vanessa pulled away from his touch and stepped back, holding her arms against her chest. "The accident wasn't your fault," she said stiffly, deliberately misunderstanding him.

Shane jammed his hands into the pockets of his jeans, watching her through hooded eyes. "We need to talk."

"Yes," she said, avoiding his eyes.

He ran a hand through his hair, tousling his dark curls. "Listen," he said abruptly. "Go sit in the living room. I'll make us some coffee."

Nodding, Vanessa left the kitchen, the puppy trailing close behind.

The house had come to life with carefully placed furniture, pictures and plants. A new thick area rug lay on the gleaming oak floor in front of the fireplace, an overstuffed couch and two armchairs placed on its edge.

Vanessa stood at one of the windows watching the wind stir, sweeping crystalline strands of hoarfrost from trees. The air sparked as sunlight pierced thinning mists.

Why did I come? she wondered with a rising sense of panic, wishing she could leave. She didn't want to struggle to maintain a calmness she didn't feel while he told her why he didn't love her, smoothly apologizing for the way in which he had treated her. She sighed and turned away from the window, realizing she had to hear the truth, so she could put him out of her life and get on with it, empty as it would be. Sitting down on one of the armchairs, she absently petted the puppy lolling happily at her feet.

Shane came in carrying two mugs of coffee. He sat on the corner of the couch nearest her chair and handed one of the mugs to her. "Lots of milk, no sugar," he said.

"Thank you." She warmed her hands on the mug, taking a welcome sip.

"How are you feeling?" he asked.

She stared at the swirling pattern in the rug under her feet. Hurt, she thought, raw. Do you even care? "Better," she said. "I'll be back at school in a day or two."

"The kids'll be glad. Tommy says the substitute is crabby."

Suddenly it was too much to bear, sitting beside him, sipping coffee and exchanging polite remarks. She wished she could feel anger, anything but this dull acceptance, waiting for him to deliver the final blow. She should be lacing into him, telling him how much she resented the way he had treated her, but she couldn't find the strength. She had been crazy to come.

"I've got to go," she said, putting her mug down with an abruptness that caused coffee to slosh over onto the glass-topped table. "I shouldn't have come."

Shane's hand snaked out and closed around her wrist. "Wait," he said. "Don't go. I've got a lot of explaining to do. Please—stay and listen."

Vanessa jerked her hand from his grasp, averting her head from the intensity of his eyes. "I don't want to hear it, Shane."

"At least let me apologize."

She looked at him, her eyes shadowed with pain. "It's gone long past the time for an apology," she said wearily, standing up. "I'm leaving." She ignored the puppy scampering around her feet and started to walk away.

"I love you, Vanessa."

The low, intensely spoken words stopped her and she spun around to face him. "You—*love* me?" Her voice rose with indignation. "You can say that after the way you treated me?" Her eyes flashed with anger. "You walked out on me, Shane, without a word—not a phone call, a letter—nothing! You knew how I felt—you had to know how much you hurt me. How dare you say you love me? You don't know the meaning of the word!"

"Then show me, Vanessa," he said intently. "I know I treated you badly—I know I can't take back the pain I caused you. But please give me a chance to try to make it up to you. Let me explain."

Vanessa stood where she was, arms crossed over her chest and head held high. "I'm listening," she said curtly.

Shane leaned forward, arms resting on his thighs. "That night we stayed here," he began, his eyes sweeping to the floor beside the hearth and darkening in memory, "I realized it was love we had shared, not just sex like it had been with others in the past. I knew that no one would ever feel as—right, as you did in my arms. I knew then how much I loved you."

Vanessa slowly made her way back to her chair and sat down again, hope slowly dispelling anger. "So why did you leave me like that?" she asked with a touch of asperity.

"I—panicked," he admitted with difficulty, a rueful light in his eyes. "I held you in my arms that night, knowing that's where I wanted you, always. And that meant marriage. I couldn't offer you anything less." He paused, his eyes darkening as he frowned. "All I could hear was my parents screaming at each other, day in and day out, and my father throwing up his hands and asking the same question just before he'd storm out of the house—'Why the hell did I ever marry you in the first place?'"

Vanessa put a hand on Shane's and squeezed gently. "That was them, Shane, not us."

"I knew that, rationally." He sighed. "But I kept thinking that they must have loved one another in the beginning and wondered what could have happened to change that love into the bitterness, the hatred, I grew up with. What was there to prevent it from happening to us? I couldn't push aside that—that primal reasoning, Vanessa, and I panicked." His lips twitched in a dry smile. "I can't think of another word for it."

"You should have talked to me about it," Vanessa said. "It wasn't fair of you to leave me like that." Her voice was low with the remnants of pain.

"I know, sweetheart, I know." He took her hand in his and held it firmly, his thumb moving in soft stroking circles on her skin. "I was letting those damned childhood ghosts ruin everything for me, even my one chance to be truly happy. I realized I needed time to confront those ghosts and put them to rest for once and for all. I had to accept that my parents' failures and inadequacies weren't mine. Can you understand, Vanessa? Can you forgive me?"

"Of course," she said gently. She moved to sit beside him on the couch, smiling softly at him. "Tommy said you were away—where did you go?"

"Halifax—to see my father." His words were unexpected. "I realized I needed to talk to him in order to free myself from the past so I would be free to love you...to marry you." He caught the look of love in her eyes. "Don't look at me like that, sweetheart," he said roughly. "Or I won't be able to finish."

Vanessa smiled and laid a hand against the side of his face, feeling joy and confidence grow in her heart. "Go on," she said softly.

Shane turned his face, pressing a kiss onto the palm of her hand. "When I got to Halifax, I found my father in the hospital about to undergo heart surgery. That's one of the reasons I was gone as long as I was."

"Oh, Shane! Is he all right?"

"He's fine now—everything went well," Shane assured her. "He's well on his way to a complete recovery. We had a long talk," he continued. "Several, actually. Somehow the circumstances made it easier. Maybe because we both knew that it might be the last chance we'd even have to clear things up between us. And once I was able to let go of my stubborn adolescent grudges, I found a man I like and admire."

"I'm glad, Shane."

He smiled. "So am I. Anyway, he told me about his marriage to my mother...things I didn't know before. He said they married not for love, but because my mother was pregnant—she miscarried shortly after the wedding, and I guess they both started to feel trapped by it all. By the time they realized they should separate, I was on the way and they made the classic mistake, staying together for my sake. The end result was the bitterness I grew up with. They both loved me—they just grew to hate the sight of each other." His lips twisted slightly and he gave his head a little shake. "I'm able to see it a little more objectively now—it's a sad story, really, the two of them staying together for all the wrong reasons, and me caught in the middle.''

"Is he happy now?" Vanessa asked.

Shane nodded. "He is. Irene—his wife—is a lovely woman. He told me that when he met her, he could no longer bear the emptiness of his life with my mother. It wasn't easy to hear, but for the first time I was able to understand. I told him about you, about the doubts I had . . .''

"And did he lay them to rest?"

"I think so." His eyes searched her, promise in their light-gray depths. "I know so," he amended softly. "Will you marry me, Vanessa?"

Her eyes brimmed with tears of happiness. "Yes, Shane," she whispered. "I'll marry you."

He pulled her into his arms, rubbing his cheek against her hair, and let out a shaky breath. "I was afraid I'd gone too far, hurt you too much," he murmured. "I was afraid you'd stopped loving me."

"I was hurt," she admitted. "And angry. But I never stopped loving you, not for a minute." She raised her head and smiled mistily at him. "I never could."

"The feeling is mutual, lovely lady," he said roughly. He laid his lips on hers, his kiss soft with love and promise.

"Mm," Vanessa murmured, smiling as he raised his head and looked at her with love glowing in his eyes, seeming more handsome than he had ever been. The sight of him took her breath away—and caused a tiny stirring of panic. She would never be the only woman who thought so. Would there come a time when he would begin to respond to looks of admiration with obvious interest?

Shane read the flickerings of doubt on her face. "What is it, sweetheart?" he asked, gently stroking her hair. "Don't hold back—tell me now."

She pushed back a bit and looked at him, wondering how to start. She sighed. "I need to tell you about Todd," she said finally.

Shane nodded. "I'm listening."

She was silent for a moment, collecting her thoughts. "Todd loved me," she said. "Enough to marry me, but—" She stopped and bit her bottom lip, unsure of how to continue. "He couldn't resist the—the lure of women who found him attractive." Her lashes swept up and she looked at Shane directly, her lips forming a wry smile. "And you, my love have many of those same attractions." She rubbed a finger along the cleft in his chin. "I'd be happier if you weren't quite so handsome," she confessed a little self-consciously. "I'm—I'm so afraid it might happen all over again."

"It won't," Shane assured her. "Never."

"How can you be so sure?" she asked, remnants of an old pain shadowing her eyes.

"Because your love means everything to me," Shane answered. "Because I know no one will ever feel as right as you do in my arms." He kissed her softly. "I'm not Todd, to be tempted by some fleeting burst of sexual pleasure that could destroy what we have, my love. I want to marry you, raise a family with you, grow old with you…loving you and only you all the years in between. I promise you that, love."

"Oh, Shane," Vanessa whispered. She buried her face in his shoulder and clung tightly, shaken by the love she saw in his eyes. His arms closed around her and he rubbed his chin against her hair.

"Okay now?" he asked.

She pushed back a bit and nodded with a warm, loving smile. "You know, Shane—I'd like to see what you've done to the rest of the house." She took his hand in hers, her voice dropping to a whisper as her lashes fanned against the flush rising in her cheeks. "I'm especially interested in the upstairs."

He tightened his fingers around her hand and stood up, pulling her with him. "Then let me take you on a guided tour," he said, leading her toward the stairs. "I think we'll start with the master bedroom."

Vanessa followed willingly, her heartbeat quickened with love and anticipation. He took her in his arms the moment they entered the room, his lips crushing against hers, sparking instant, heated response.

Clothing was stripped off as they fell upon the bed, hands, mouths, bodies meeting, melding, moving in urgent passion. With a loud cry Vanessa arched to his moan of release, feeling her own ecstasy radiate outward in dizzying waves.

Shane cradled her in his arms, stroking the damp hair back from her face. "That was fast," he said, his eyes laughing.

"I'm not complaining." Vanessa smiled, moving her body, luxuriatingly heavy with satisfaction, against his. "We're good together, Shane," she said, running her hands over the rippling muscles on his back.

"Damned good," he agreed readily, kissing her. "Tell me," he murmured against her mouth, "when can we get married?"

"Soon," she promised, pursing her lips in a kiss.

"How soon—tomorrow? Next week?" he persisted.

Vanessa gave a soft little laugh. "Can this be the same man who was so deathly afraid of marriage?" she teased.

"I discovered I'm more afraid of life without you," he said, his eyes darkening. "I love you too much to ever be without you again."

Vanessa buried her head in his shoulder and held him tight. "I love you so much, Shane."

He felt the scald of tears against his skin and pushed her back, an expression of alarm on his face. "You're crying," he said, dismayed.

Vanessa smiled and shook her head, wiping away the tears. "I'm just happy," she assured him with a kiss.

Shane's arms tightened around her, his cheek resting against her hair. "So am I, sweetheart," he murmured. "So am I."

She played with the hair curling on the back of his neck. "Any remaining doubts?" she asked.

"None," he said with conviction. "Absolutely none. Nothing has ever felt right as this."

"It does feel right, doesn't it?" She sighed happily, rubbing her cheek against the warm, smooth skin of his chest. "Promise me something, Shane...if you ever start feeling doubtful again about us—just take me to bed and we'll talk it out after."

His eyes gleamed. "After what?"

She pressed her face into the crook of his neck and placed short kisses along his jaw. "After we make love," she whispered. Her soft hands moved over him, caressing lovingly.

Shane groaned softly, relishing her touch. "I think I feel some of those doubts stirring now," he said, cupping the curve of her hips and pulling her closer to him.

Vanessa's brows arched and she smiled at him, running a finger down the bridge of his nose. "It's not doubts that I feel stirring, Shane Wilder," she said, her face soft with laughter as she moved against him.

He stroked her satin skin leisurely, his eyes darkening with desire and closing as his mouth found hers. His kiss was long and hard. "I love you, Vanessa," he murmured against the throbbing softness of her lips.

"And I love you, Shane," she whispered shakily.

"Always?" he asked intently.

"Always," she promised.

Temptation™

TEMPTATION WILL BE
EVEN HARDER TO RESIST...

In September, Temptation is presenting a sophisticated new face to the world. A fresh look that truly brings Harlequin's most intimate romances into focus.

What's more, all-time favorite authors Barbara Delinsky, Rita Clay Estrada, Jayne Ann Krentz and Vicki Lewis Thompson will join forces to help us celebrate. The result? A very special quartet of Temptations...

- **Four striking covers**
- **Four stellar authors**
- **Four sensual love stories**
- **Four variations on one spellbinding theme**

All in one great month! Give in to Temptation in September.

TDESIGN-1

ATTRACTIVE, SPACE SAVING BOOK RACK

Display your most prized novels on this handsome and sturdy book rack. The hand-rubbed walnut finish will blend into your library decor with quiet elegance, providing a practical organizer for your favorite hard-or soft-covered books.

Only $9.95

Approximately 16" x 8" when assembled

Assembles in seconds!

To order, rush your name, address and zip code, along with a check or money order for $10.70* ($9.95 plus 75¢ postage and handling) payable to *Harlequin Reader Service*:

Harlequin Reader Service
Book Rack Offer
901 Fuhrmann Blvd.
P.O. Box 1396
Buffalo, NY 14269-1396

Offer not available in Canada.

BKR-1A

*New York and Iowa residents add appropriate sales tax.

Harlequin Intrigue

Two exciting new stories each month.

Each title mixes a contemporary, sophisticated romance with the surprising twists and turns of a puzzler...romance with "something more."

Because romance can be quite an adventure.

Intrg-1

Romance, Suspense and Adventure